P. P.

W9-BES-685

His hands moved lightly on her hips

Shane bent his head, and his mouth was upon hers. There was only the softness and warmth of his lips, the heat that fanned her body, the tremulous paralyzing sensations that pulsed in pinpoints of lights behind her closed eyes and abruptly stilled everything within her—her breath, her heartbeat, her will and her reason. It was more than Lauren had ever imagined.

When he drew away, slowly, reluctantly, almost cautiously, she felt stunned and weak. He said softly, "That was definitely worth waiting for."

Her mouth throbbed with the warmth of his. This was Shane Holt, the man of magical words and legendary music...he could have any woman he wanted. This was the man who'd despised her from the moment they'd met. None of it made sense!

WELCOME
TO THE WONDERFUL WORLD
OF *Harlequin Presents*

Interesting, informative and entertaining,
each Harlequin romance portrays an appealing
and original love story. With a varied array
of settings, we may lure you on an African safari,
to a quaint Welsh village, or an exotic Riviera
location—anywhere and everywhere that adventurous
men and women fall in love.

As publishers of Harlequin romances, we're
extremely proud of our books. Since 1949,
Harlequin Enterprises has built its publishing
reputation on the solid base of quality and
originality. Our stories are the most popular
paperback romances sold in North America; every
month, eight new titles are released and sold at
nearly every book-selling store in Canada and the
United States.

A free catalogue listing all available Harlequin romances
can be yours by writing to the

HARLEQUIN READER SERVICE
1440 South Priest Drive, Tempe, AZ 85281
Canadian address: Stratford, Ontario N5A 6W2

We sincerely hope you enjoy reading
this Harlequin Presents.

Yours truly,

THE PUBLISHERS

REBECCA FLANDERS

morning song

Harlequin Books

TORONTO • NEW YORK • LONDON
AMSTERDAM • PARIS • SYDNEY • HAMBURG
STOCKHOLM • ATHENS • TOKYO • MILAN

Harlequin Presents first edition October 1983
ISBN 0-373-10632-7

Original hardcover edition published in 1983
by Mills & Boon Limited

Copyright © 1983 by Rebecca Flanders. All rights reserved.
Philippine copyright 1983. Australian copyright 1983.
Except for use in any review, the reproduction or utilization of
this work in whole or in part in any form by any electronic,
mechanical or other means, now known or hereafter invented,
including xerography, photocopying and recording, or in any
information storage or retrieval system, is forbidden without
the permission of the publisher, Harlequin Enterprises Limited,
225 Duncan Mill Road, Don Mills, Ontario, Canada M3B 3K9.

All the characters in this book have no existence outside the
imagination of the author and have no relation whatsoever to
anyone bearing the same name or names. They are not even
distantly inspired by any individual known or unknown to the
author, and all the incidents are pure invention.

The Harlequin trademarks, consisting of the words
HARLEQUIN PRESENTS and the portrayal of a Harlequin,
are trademarks of Harlequin Enterprises Limited and are
registered in the Canada Trade Marks Office; the portrayal
of a Harlequin is registered in the United States Patent
and Trademark Office.

Printed in U.S.A.

CHAPTER ONE

LAUREN DAVIS watched the headlights of what must have been the sixth car pull into the circular drive below and then dim, and she shuddered and stepped away from the window. A few friends, Marie had said. She had already counted eighteen laughing, well-dressed people getting out of their cars and going into the house, and the party had not yet really begun.

The last thing Lauren felt like tonight was a party, and she had protested as much to Marie. She had only arrived at Marie and Marvin Van Fossen's Colorado home this afternoon and she still was not quite certain what she was doing here. She was certain that she was in no mood for socialising, as Marie should know very well.

She was ashamed of the small sense of resentment she felt rising for her host and hostess. Van and Marie had gone beyond the call of duty for her in the last few months and she should have been grateful. Van had flown to New York less than a week after Lauren's surgery—though how he had found out about it Lauren still did not know—and had visited her every day in the hospital. He had tried to cheer her with commonsense advice and small talk and had even, without her asking, known exactly what things to bring from her apartment to make her hospital stay more comfortable. He tried, in his very low-key way, to convince her that her life was not over simply because her stage career was. Of course he had not succeeded in that: he simply did not understand.

With a martyred sigh, Lauren wandered over to the mirror and took a long hard look at herself. She was appalled. Why had she never noticed before how much weight she had lost? She was wearing a plum-coloured sweater which she had intended to match with a long grey skirt, and panties, and her reflection in the mirror looked emaciated. Her thighs were no bigger than a child's, and as she lifted her arm to brush her honey-coloured hair the sweater rode up to reveal the sharp point of her hipbone. Even through the wool sweater she could see the outline of fragile ribs and her chest was as flat as a boy's. Selfconsciously, she brought her hand to her breasts and wondered how she could have possibly ignored how awful she looked before tonight. The semi-circular scar on her knee was purplish-red and huge, and she refused, she absolutely *refused* to go to a party looking like this.

She drew on a robe and went over to the bed, curling her legs beneath her and propping the pillows behind her shoulders. She felt relieved, for now she had a concrete excuse to give Marie. She reached for her cassette player and felt an unfamiliar sense of contentment steal over her as she prepared to indulge herself in that last fantasy she had left, music.

For the past ten years she had sought solace and found her greatest pleasure in the same way. Van had known exactly what she needed most while she was in the hospital, and on his first visit had brought her tape player and her Shane Holt tapes. Throughout those nightmarish days she had only to press a switch and through the music a man she did not know spoke to her and comforted her, and seemed to understand her better than she did herself. She had sublet her New York apartment when Van insisted upon carrying her off to Colorado for the winter, and the only thing she had saved from the remnants of her past life was her collection of Shane Holt tapes. She put one into the machine now and leaned back and closed her eyes, letting the music and the lyrics carry her once again into a world outside herself.

But the respite was all too brief. There was a sharp rap on the door and Marie came in.

Lauren gave a sheepish grin as she switched off the

tape player. 'I tried to tell you,' she explained before her hostess could say anything, 'I really don't feel like a party.'

Marie, with her hands on her black velvet-clad hips, demanded, 'And why not?'

Lauren shrugged uncomfortably. Obviously, this was not going to be as easy as she had planned. 'All those strangers—I just feel awkward, that's all.'

'This, from a girl who's faced an audience of over a thousand almost every night of her life?' exclaimed Marie in disdain. 'Sheer nonsense! I'm warning you, young lady, I won't take no for an answer, so you may as well get up and get dressed or I'll come over there and do it myself.'

Lauren knew she was not being fair to Marie, and this was certainly no way to express her gratitude for all that Marie and Van had done for her over the years. The two families had been friends almost since before Lauren was born, when Van had produced a record by the orchestra of which both Lauren's parents were members. When an automobile accident had taken Lauren's parents when she was twenty, Van and Marie had stepped naturally into the surrogate role, comforting, supporting, seeing her through the worst. They attended all her openings and made certain she never lacked for anything; they loved her like a daughter, and Lauren returned the affection. Now that tragedy had struck Lauren again they were here to stand by her and offer all they could to ease the pain. Even though their efforts were in vain, Lauren knew she could have at least made an attempt to show them that she appreciated their concern.

Lauren got up with a sigh. 'None of my clothes fit,' she complained. 'I don't have anything to wear. I'll feel stupid and tongue-tied, and I'll ruin your party.'

To prove her point, she stepped out of her robe and held up the skirt she had intended to wear with her sweater. It did not take more than a glance to notice the uncomplimentary effect of the outfit, but Marie looked her over critically. 'Perhaps,' she decided tactfully, 'sweaters aren't the most flattering thing for you right now. I'm sure you have a pretty blouse somewhere . . .'

Lauren gave a helpless little laugh as Marie began rifling through her closet. She pulled out one of Lauren's favourite blouses—a white chiffon spangled with gold. The full sleeves were three-quarter length, and the deep lace inset trimmed with ruffles hid the most obvious defects of her figure. Marie chose a pair of wool slacks in a rich cranberry colour—they hung on Lauren, but they were the newly fashionable baggy style, so it was not noticeable. Marie hurried along the dressing process, complaining, 'I'll have you know I'm a very good hostess, and everyone loves my parties. This is the first time in my life I've ever had to practically drag two of my house guests by their ears to one of my parties, and I'll tell you right now, I don't much like the feeling!'

Lauren pulled back her hair with ivory combs and tried to hide her pained expression with a rather false smile. That was another thing that had intimidated and disappointed her about this trip. She had accepted Van's invitation because a few months in his secluded mountain home had sounded like exactly what she wanted—isolation, privacy, no demands and no pressures. She had forgotten that while Van's home was secluded it was hardly isolated, and rarely did more than a week pass at a time without house guests. She should not have been surprised when Marie had told her as soon as she arrived that she would be sharing their hospitality with another friend of theirs for a few days. Lauren had seen no sign of the other guest during the afternoon, though, and, if Marie's statement about his reluctance to attend the party could be given any credence, perhaps he was just as anxious to preserve his privacy as she was hers. She hoped so. The party was bad enough; she did not think she could bear to try to make small talk with a stranger for days at a time.

When she was finally downstairs, Lauren discovered

she had been right; she did feel awkward and shy in a room filled with strangers. Although everyone to whom she was introduced was very polite, she found her usual gift for witty conversation had suddenly disappeared. Most of the guests were friends and associates of Van's from the music business, a lively group whose company Lauren would have usually enjoyed. But tonight she did not have anything to say, her mind was a blank, and she was relieved when her new acquaintances made polite excuses after a few moments and left her alone. She felt as though everyone noticed her limp, and the more she tried to hide it, the worse it became. She wished she had worn more make-up, a different outfit . . . she wished she had stayed in her room.

A nice-looking young man to whom she had been introduced only a few moments before came over to her. 'The lady looks like she could use a drink,' he smiled, and pressed a glass into her hand.

Lauren could not hide her surprise over the fact that he had returned, and she accepted the glass with murmured thanks.

He continued to smile at her. 'So what are you doing standing over here all by yourself? A pretty girl like you can't be shy.'

'I—I'm not much for parties,' Lauren replied, keeping her eyes on her glass. She wished he would go away.

'Well, I know just the cure for that.' He took her arm. 'Let's dance.'

She shrank back in a quick rush of alarm. 'N-no,' she stammered, casting frantically about for some means of escape. 'I—don't dance, I——'

He laughed and tightened his persuasive hold on her arm. 'Come on, sweetheart, you can't pull that on me. Marie has already told me you're a professional dancer, so let's get out there and show them how it's done.' He tugged on her arm. 'Let's boogie!'

She pulled her arm away. Her heart was pounding and her cheeks were red, but she managed with as much dignity as possible, 'I can't dance. I—had an accident. I . . .' her voice sank to almost a whisper, 'can't dance.'

He looked at her for a moment as though she had suddenly turned into a freak before his eyes, and to her shame she felt angry tears sting her eyelids. She looked up at him defiantly anyway, and hated the look of embarrassment and annoyance that came over his face. 'Okay, baby, pardon me for asking.' There was a hint of sarcasm beneath the defensiveness in his tone as he turned away. 'All you had to say was no, you know,' he shot back over his shoulder, and Lauren watched him push his way through the crowd with a sense of overwhelming despair.

What was she doing here in the midst of all these people, the gaiety, the artificial brightness, the laughter and the music . . .? She did not belong here. She was a cripple, a freak, and had she really thought for one moment that 'nice' young man would understand? No, these were the Beautiful People, the whole and healthy good-time people, and anyone and anything less than perfect was repulsive in their eyes. She did not belong here.

She edged herself into a corner, out of sight and she hoped out of mind. She sipped her drink and watched the activity around her. Once this had been her world, but it was no longer. Had Marie really thought *this* would make her feel better? Not one person in this room had anything more important on his mind than who he was going home with, and a chasm as wide as the Grand Canyon separated Lauren from the rest of them. *They* had never known fear or despair or the aching emptiness which dawned with every new day. They had never seen their dreams crushed to rubble or faced a future devoid of promise. They did not know, not one of them, what it was like to lose in a gamble with fate.

She was just weighing her chances of making a discreet exit by way of the stairs when Van spotted her and waved. Her spirits sank as he came over to her.

'Come on,' he insisted, taking her arm, 'there's someone I want you to meet.'

'Do you mean there's someone I've missed?' she sighed, and he laughed goodnaturedly as he led her across the room.

They approached two men in conversation—at least, one of them was in conversation. He was an older man, balding and a little paunchy in an outrageously printed silk shirt with a heavy gold chain about his neck, and his thin voice raised in disgust and recrimination reached Lauren long before they were close enough to be introduced. 'I tell you, man, it baffles me, I mean really *baffles* me. You want to try to explain it to me one more time? You want to try to explain to me how those six-figure royalties just turn you off and how the thought of a gold record makes you sick to your stomach? How you never really liked all those gorgeous broads crawling all over you and your fancy sports cars and that swinging pad you used to keep in N.Y.C.? Whatever happened to that Lamborghini you were going to buy, anyway? I tell you, man, I just don't understand it . . .' The voice became a whine. 'We had some good times together, you know what I mean? Some really good times. And so now what are you trying to be, some kind of Messiah or something? I mean, it's your own trip, man, but how about remembering your friends on the way? We could have it good all over again . . .'

The man he was addressing was younger, dressed in jeans, a white turtleneck sweater, and a blue corduroy jacket. His eyes were very cold and his face was hard. He said quietly, 'Why don't you go to hell, Marty?'

Lauren would have liked at that moment to discreetly walk away, but Van felt no compunction about breaking into what was obviously a personal and potentially explosive argument. He said cheerfully, 'Are you still giving our boy a hard time, Marty? I'm going to stop inviting you to my parties if you don't lower the volume on your hard sell!'

The one called Marty managed to look disgruntled and despairing at the same time. 'Why don't you try to talk some sense into him?' he demanded of Van. 'A whole life shot down the tubes, and does he care? Not him, no sir. And what about me?' he demanded plaintively of the man in jeans. 'Do you know what ten per cent of nothing is? Nothing, that's what.' He threw his hands up in the air at the stony lack of response and walked away, muttering something about 'gratitude' and 'loyalty'.

'A discontented ex-manager,' Van explained to Lauren, and drew her forward. For a moment he paused, almost as though for dramatic effect, and there was a hint of an excited secret in his voice as she said, 'Lauren, this is Shane Holt. Shane, this is the girl Marie was telling you about, Lauren Davis. Since you'll be sharing the same roof for a while, you should get to know one another.'

Lauren looked at him. A year ago she would have fallen to her knees and worshipped the very ground on which this man walked—even six months ago she would not have been ashamed to admit that she was stricken with a very adolescent case of hero-worship. For Shane Holt was no ordinary man; he was not even an ordinary hero.

During the height of his career he had been billed as a soft rock singer by some; a pop artist by others. Actually, he was a folk singer in the truest, most basic sense of the word. The songs he wrote told the story of everyday life wrapped into universal themes with a brilliance the greatest novelist or poet who had ever lived could only envy. He sang of the innocence of childhood and the beauty of growing old, the poignancy of first love remembered, the simple harmony of death. He sang about life on the road and the dark, lonely thoughts that haunt the midnight hours. With words and music he painted unforgettable portraits of slices of life rich with meaning—the fisherman bringing in his haul on a cold, stormy day;

the father and son walking quietly through autumn woods; the mother waiting patiently for her children to come home. His gift of language and rhyme was extraordinary, almost in the calibre of classical poets, and his style was unmistakable. Lauren knew that he had a graduate degree from Princeton and was a Rhodes Scholar, and that he had gone into music against the will of his family, but other than that little was known about him. He kept his private life very private. Perhaps it was his genius and his background which set him apart in the music world, but to Lauren it was something more—a sensitivity, a rare quality of understanding life in all its beauty and expressing that understanding with the precise words and melody which made it real.

He had produced three albums in five years, and from each of them he had no fewer than four singles to make the top twenty on the popular charts. Strangely, none of his songs ever climbed above twenty in popularity, but they hovered at that number and fell slowly. He was not really a teen idol—in fact, his following, according to one music magazine, had been almost cultish in nature—and he made no effort to compete with the flash-in-the-pan hard rock tunes which were constantly bombarding the charts. His songs rose with dignity above the trash, held their positions solidly for a respectable lifetime, and then faded just as gracefully from the public ear. Even though he had not made a recording in almost five years, his songs were still considered classics. Lauren discovered something new in them every time she listened.

She had seen him only once in concert. He had held the audience mesmerised in his spell for over two hours while he told his stories and painted his pictures in song, and at the end she had thought the building would collapse under the wild thunder of endless applause. Her own hands had hurt from clapping and tears were in her eyes as Shane Holt got up quietly and left the stage. Throughout the performance he had not said a word, but let his music speak for him. Yet he had touched his audience in a way Lauren had never dreamed possible. It was the best show she had ever seen.

At that time his dark blond hair had been worn below his shoulders and he had a full blond beard. She was not surprised that she had not recognised him now. The beard was gone, and his hair seemed darker in colour, almost brown, clipped just above the collar and swept to the side. There was something different about the eyes, too, which were a foggy hazel colour, and about his face. But Lauren had only seen him that once, and from the distance which separated the stage from the third row orchestra, and she could not be sure what, exactly, it was about his appearance which seemed to be disappointing.

'I hardly think that's necessary,' he was saying to Van now, 'as I won't be here long enough to need to get to know anyone.' His eyes flickered over Lauren once, without interest, and then away. 'I've already stayed longer than I planned.'

'Shane usually spends a month or two out of every summer with us,' Van explained to Lauren, and Lauren looked at him in surprise.

'You never mentioned it,' she said.

'That's because,' Shane Holt answered for him in a rather cool tone, 'he's too good a friend to jeopardise my privacy.'

Lauren stared at him. She did not know what she had expected from him, but this coolness, the distant manner which bordered on rudeness, took her by surprise. It was totally out of place for the sensitive, gentle man she had known him to be.

Van placed a hand on each of their shoulders and smiled benevolently. 'Well, now that I've matched you each with the perfect partner for the evening, I'll leave you alone. You two have a lot in common, you'll see. Misery loves company!'

Lauren made a gesture of protest, but he moved too fast for her. She was left alone with the man she had been in love with most of her adult life, and she wished she was any place else.

She should have been impressed. This was a dream come true, the chance of a lifetime, she was standing face to face with the man whose work she had treasured for ten years, whose soul she knew so well it had almost become a part of her. There should have been a hundred questions she wanted to ask him, she should have been bursting with things to say to him. So many times she had sighed to herself that she would die content if only she could walk up and shake the hand of the genius who had created such beauty ... Just to pay homage, just to say 'Thank you' for the glimpse he had given her of art in its most perfect form. But all of that seemed so distant now, none of it appropriate. It was as though, since the accident, a dull cloud had filmed over every emotion she had ever had, and all she could think of to say was, 'I liked you better with your beard.'

He replied, without looking at her, 'Thank you for that information. I'm taking a poll.'

She was almost shocked into some sharp retort of her own, but as a matter of fact, she was too taken aback to think of one. But some of her lethargy lifted as she bristled with insult, and she told him coldly, 'There's no need to be rude. I was just making conversation.' And she turned on her heel to go.

'I wasn't being rude,' he replied in a bored tone, and she stopped. 'I was just being miserable. I believe that's one of the things we're supposed to have in common.'

She turned back to him, not so much because she wanted to stay as because she did not want to think of his eyes upon her as she limped across the room. He watched the activity across the room and did not appear to be much interested in whether she stayed or not.

After a moment, Lauren tried again to make conversation. 'Have you known Van long?'

He made a noncommittal sound and sipped his drink, not looking at her. He seemed to have a real problem with making eye contact, and it annoyed her. It was her opinion that people who refused to look you in the eye were generally hiding something, and that was something she simply would not have expected from him. So, she thought wryly, your idol has feet of clay—don't they all?

Then he said unexpectedly, 'Do you want to dance?'

She recoiled from him as though struck, and her response was swift and sharp. 'No!' It was a self-protective instinct, that was all, an automatic reaction which was completely uncontrollable.

He lifted one brow slightly and mimicked her words softly, 'You don't have to be rude; I was just trying to make conversation.'

She swallowed back a furious scarlet flush of embarrassment. She wanted to turn and walk away, but she would not give him the satisfaction. Instead, she faced him squarely, painted a pleasant expression on her face, and pretended to ignore their last interchange. She commented casually, 'I know your music.'

He dropped his eyes to his glass and repeated softly, 'You know my music.' The slight twist of his lips was derogatory, and the tone of his voice mocking. 'Well, at least you didn't say, "I've bought every record you ever made, Mr Holt", or "Gee, I think you're just terrific, Mr Holt." Thanks for small favours.'

She felt anger surge another stain of colour to her face. Was this the real Shane Holt, the man behind the sensitive lyrics and gentle prose—arrogant, conceited, sarcastic? She would never have believed it, and she did not feel so much disappointed at that moment as furious. He might very well be the most brilliant musician of the twentieth century—and right now she was not so sure any more—but he had no right to talk to her like that . . . to treat anyone as no more than dust beneath his feet. She said stiffly, her eyes flashing a muted warning, 'I'm not another one of your groupies,

Mr Holt, which I'm sure will come as a terrible disappointment to you. I was merely trying to——'

'Make conversation, I know,' he interrupted drily. 'Yet you presume to say you know my music. For your further enlightenment, Miss—whatever-your-name-was, let me tell you that no one knows my music. My producer doesn't know it, my fans don't know it, certainly the radio people don't know it. I don't even know it myself. So save yourself from making the same embarrassing mistake twice and never assume you think you know anything about an artist's work.'

If misery loved company, he had certainly bargained for his share of it tonight! He had engaged her in battle and he was not going to escape unscathed. Lauren felt adrenalin start to flow for the first time in months. 'On the contrary,' she replied mildly, her eyes still glittering, 'it would be difficult to assume anything about your work, since you haven't recorded anything in five years. In fact, I'm amazed that *you* presume to speak in the present tense about it at all. Isn't that all just ancient history?'

He was unruffled, and that only annoyed her more. 'Perhaps,' he agreed, and sipped from his glass.

'So,' she demanded, and this was one of the questions she had promised herself she would ask him if ever she was honoured—honoured!—to meet him, 'what have you been doing these past years?' She remembered how anxiously she had waited at first for his next album release, how disappointed she had been when it never came, and how she had wondered, the way the ignominious do about the famous, what had happened to him. He seemed to have abruptly disappeared off the face of the earth with no explanation or excuses, and she had even thought at one point he might have been dead. No one with the enormous talent he had could simply wilfully stop creating, and she thought he might have run into trouble with contracts or recording studios or producers . . . she had never dreamed that the mystery of the disappearance of her idol could be solved by simply asking Van.

And so it came as a surprise to her when he replied simply, without looking at her, 'Nothing.'

'Nothing!' she repeated incredulously, unable to keep her genuine shock from showing on her face, superseding all other emotions of spite and anger.

'Nothing,' he repeated blandly, and set his drink on the table. 'Now, if you'll excuse me . . .'

'I will not!' she cried, and caught his arm without thinking. She thought of the wasted talent, the rare gift tossed so carelessly aside, the breathtaking prose and the heartrending melodies she would never hear again because he had decided to do—nothing! And, irrationally, she thought of how she would have given the world to be free to perform her art and how he so casually dismissed his own freedom to do so and she was furious. For the first time since the accident she was actually enraged over something other than her own fate, and Shane Holt received the full force of it. 'I will *not* excuse you,' she reiterated in a low, seething voice. His eyes fastened pointedly and with some surprise upon the grip she had on his arm and she released it automatically, but went on, her eyes snapping, 'How can you say so casually you've done "nothing"? Do you mean you haven't written, you haven't performed—all these years we've been waiting for something new from you and you've done *nothing*?'

'Miss——?' he paused politely.

'Lauren,' she snapped, impatient for his response to her accusations. 'Lauren Davis.'

'All right, Lauren,' he said smoothly. 'While I must say I'm flattered that you've been waiting all this time with bated breath for my next plunge into musical genius, please allow me to advise you not to wait too much longer. And I might also point out that what I've been doing with my time for the past five years is, quite simply, none of your business.'

'It *is* my business!' she retorted, highly incensed. 'It's the business of everyone who ever heard you sing and loved your music. You can't just throw it away! You have an obligation——'

'I have nothing,' he interrupted shortly, and then the sharp lines on his face smoothed out into a martyred sigh and he suggested, 'But if you insist upon finishing this incredibly boring conversation could we at least do it in a more ventilated area? I might be able to tolerate your presence for a few more minutes, but if I don't get out of this room pretty soon I'll certainly choke on the smoke.'

She glared at him. 'Were you always such a bastard, or is it a recent refinement?'

'Recent,' he admitted mildly, and started across the room.

Lauren did not hesitate about accompanying him. She was selfconscious about the limp, which was made even worse by the high-heeled sandals she was wearing. Shane Holt noticed her difficulty and slowed his gait, but that only embarrassed her and annoyed her more.

The noise and bright gaiety of the party receded into the cool, clear night as they crossed the flagstone porch. He started down the steps towards the still, silent lawn, and she followed him. But on the first step she tripped, or her knee simply gave way, and she muffled a cry as she started to fall.

His clasp on her elbow was firm and warm, easily guiding her to her own sense of balance again. He inquired, 'Are you all right?'

She bit her lip against pain and humiliation and managed briefly, 'Yes.'

'I noticed you were limping.' There was a new inflection to his voice now, or perhaps it was simply the absence of his customary sarcasm. Lauren was too embarrassed and too impatient with herself to care one way or the other. 'What's wrong?'

'Nothing.' She drew her arm away quickly. 'It's nothing.'

'Do you want to sit down?'

'No!' her retort was sharp, her posture stiff. 'I told you, it's nothing. I'm fine.'

He looked at her for a moment, then he said casually,

'Then you don't mind if I do.' He lowered himself gracefully to the second step, looped his arms about his knees, and simply sat there, looking peacefully out over the silent lawn. Lauren had no choice but to follow.

She still did not have full flection in her knee, and sitting, especially upon so low an object as the step, was an awkward and clumsy process at best. Shane Holt did not offer to help; in fact he did not appear to even notice her struggle, and Lauren, wrapped up in her own embarrassment and impatience, was nonetheless relieved that she did not have his mockery to contend with on top of everything else.

When she was finally settled, her right knee stretched out stiffly and somewhat uncomfortably before her, she did not trust herself to speak for a while. She was afraid he would notice what a great physical effort such a simple thing as sitting had required of her, and she did not think she could take another one of his humiliating remarks just then. So she gave herself time to regain her composure and steady her breathing by examining his profile in the shadowed reflection of the window lights.

She did not really like him better with the beard, she realised as she took the time to really look at him. He had a fine face, strong and well-defined, with character lines she had never noticed before from the album covers—or perhaps they had simply been hidden by the beard. The nose was sharp and irregular, as though it might have been broken at some time, but its slightly uneven shape only made it more interesting. His mouth was full and attractive, and she could easily imagine those lips curving into a gentle smile, only the deep lines on either side told her they did not do so often. The eyes ... it was the eyes, she realised, which had bothered her on the first meeting, which made him seem so different from his photographs and from the way she remembered him. His eyes had once been gentle and dreamy, sensuously shaded by thick lashes and possessing the perpetual hint of a far-away smile. There was a hardness there now which was incongruous with what she knew of him, and the look of a man who has seen too much too soon and cannot forget. In repose, as he was now, it was an almost haunted look, and it made her uneasy.

She had to break the silence. 'So what happened to you?' she demanded. 'Did success go to your head? Did you make so much money you got in trouble with the I.R.S.? Did you just get bored? Crack under the pressure? What?'

He stirred lazily and leaned back on one elbow, looking up at the mountains silhouetted in the crystal-clear net of stars. 'All of the above,' he replied.

Lauren shook her head firmly. 'I won't accept that. No one can just walk away from something like that. You can't just turn your back on a talent—not when it's born into you, like your love of music was.' How well, how achingly well, she knew that.

The glance he gave her in the uncertain light was sharp, but it lasted no more than a second before he turned his eyes back to the stars. And his voice was mild. 'You seem to know a great deal about me, Miss Davis.'

'I think I do,' she said softly, but she was really thinking about herself. 'Enough to know that the gift for music, the need to perform, is not something you can take up or put down at will. You see, it doesn't really belong to you at all, you belong to it, and whether or not to use it is never really your choice.'

There was a long, very still silence. Even the music which came from inside the house momentarily stopped and the tree frogs suddenly ceased their raucous chirping. But when at last Shane Holt spoke his voice was curt, and icy cold. He said, 'That's a pretty philosophy, but fortunately it doesn't apply to me. The music business didn't agree with me, so I got out, that's all.'

She could sense tension, coiled like an animal ready to spring, in every line of his body, and with each word he spoke he had seemed to withdraw further from her.

She should have been warned, a cautious person would have left well enough alone, but Lauren thought of all the songs which would remain forever unborn, all the audiences which could never be held spellbound by the magic he created, and she said, 'No.' Her voice was soft, but the firm shake of her head determined. 'You can't mean that. Not the man who wrote *Midnight Melody* and *Passages*—it was more than just a business to you. You can't just decide you don't like it any more and quit.'

His eyes glittered dangerously in the crystal starlight. 'I can,' he returned smoothly, 'do anything I like.'

She looked at him, at the hard lines of his face and the cold, distant eyes, and she did not want to believe it, but she knew it was true. The man behind the beautiful music was not a reflection of the soul of his art. She would never have thought it was possible that something so delicate and genuine could come from someone so harsh and unfeeling; it broke every rule she had ever imagined she knew about creativity and talent. And still she shook her head slowly as though fighting the obvious while she was forced to admit painfully, wonderingly, 'You're not the same. You're not the same at all.'

Shane Holt stood abruptly, fury and impatience in his eyes, and lashed back at her, 'Get that heartbroken look out of your eyes, it doesn't impress me a bit. It's not my fault that you built me up into some sort of god, and I won't be responsible for the fact that you've found the truth to be less than what you expected. What you see is what you get, and that's my final word on the subject.'

He turned sharply to go back inside, but then he looked back at her. 'You're a pesky little brat, Miss Davis,' he said darkly. 'I hope to see as little as possible of you before I leave.'

In a moment she heard the door open on the laughter and music inside, and then slam again. She drew her one knee up and wrapped her arms about it, resting her cheek against the wool of her slacks and fighting the urge to cry. She felt empty and bereft inside, as though she had just lost her best friend—or worse, as though her best friend had just betrayed her. For that was what Shane Holt had become to her, in the fantasy world of his music—her best friend. He had seen her through the dark times, he had celebrated her victories. He had promised order and meaning to life when she could not see it for herself. He had understood her as no one had ever done, he had made her believe in things untouchable—things like hope, love, a better tomorrow. Now she discovered it had all been a lie.

She wished Van had never brought her here. She wished she had never met Shane Holt, she wished she could have gone on thinking he was dead or living in Brazil or anything ... anything other than the truth. She thought of all those times when his music had been her only refuge against the black depression—when just knowing that there was someone in the world with a soul so pure and a mind so perfect had given her the strength to go on. Now she did not have anything left.

Yet he was right. *She* had built him up and made him immortal—all she had ever known of him had been a contrivance of her mind. How could she be angry with him for turning out to be human?

She wasn't angry with him, she realised bleakly, as much as she was with herself for ever having been such a fool. For a brief time this evening while fighting with him the despair which had haunted her since the accident had disappeared, but now it all came back. In the space of six months she had lost two dreams and all her illusions, and it did not seem fair.

CHAPTER TWO

By the next morning Lauren had made a cautious peace with herself regarding Shane Holt. After all, she was twenty-six years old and should have outgrown the stage of adolescent crushes years ago. She had been disappointed before, and she would not let this disillusionment crush her. Shane Holt was still the least of her problems.

Marie and Van were in the kitchen when Lauren came down, and Marie was just putting breakfast on the table. It was a bright, clear morning, as evidenced through the wide bay window which encased the breakfast area, and the mountains seemed to have moved during the night and deposited themselves right in Van's back yard. The cobalt sky and the emerald grass were the perfect frame for the riotous colours of the trees in the valley beyond—a panoramic sweep of orange, gold, scarlet, russet and purple. Those colours were reflected in the bright interior of the kitchen, which was done in the unlikely combination of orange and scarlet—orange plaid wallpaper, bright orange appliances, red pots and pans and scarlet cushions on the breakfast booth, with a pot of paper poppies on the table. The walls which weren't papered were covered with gleaming pine panelling, and the entire effect was guaranteed to chase away drowsiness and set the blood to rushing for a new day. Simply walking into the kitchen, seeing the beautiful view from the window and smelling the good breakfast smells, had the effect of vanishing all hints of depression for Lauren, and all thoughts of Shane Holt—at least temporarily.

'Well,' Marie greeted her brightly as she came in, 'I'm glad to see my party has done you no lasting harm—even though you did stay for an entire hour and fifteen minutes!'

24

Lauren laughed. 'I'm sure it was a very nice party, Marie. But I was asleep the minute my head hit the pillow—I told you I was tired.' And surprisingly enough, that was the truth. She had expected to lie tossing and turning all night over the unhappy events of the evening, but fatigue, or the strain of the past months, or perhaps simply the fresh country air, had taken its toll. She had not even dreamed about him.

Van said, placing the coffee pot on the table, 'You look better already—doesn't she, Marie? Aren't you glad you came?'

Marie said, 'She's still got a way to go before she's the rosy-cheeked girl I remember, but we'll soon fix that. Anything special for breakfast?'

'Whatever you have that's fattening,' replied Lauren, and Marie beamed.

'That's the spirit!' she said, and placed a huge platter of fresh cinammon rolls on the table. The aroma was intoxicating and Lauren was surprised to find she was actually hungry. She sat down across from Van as Marie brought a platter of bacon, scrambled eggs, and toast, and another of sliced melon and grapefruit.

Lauren groaned, 'You don't expect me to eat all that!'

'I expect you to try,' replied Marie firmly, and pushed the butter dish closer to Lauren's plate as she sat down. 'Use lots of butter,' she advised. 'It's the best way I know to put on weight.'

Lauren laughed. Marie, approaching fifty, had the figure of a girl half that age, and Lauren doubted she had ever had to count calories in her life. Lauren, however, had spent her entire life rigorously watching her weight, and she was surprised that she had to fight a small battle with guilt before determinedly adding an extra pat of butter to her cinnamon roll. It came as something of a shock to her to realise she need never look at another container of yogurt in her life, no more skipping meals when the scales tipped half a pound, no more getting up at six a.m. to do warm-ups, no more gruelling hours at the barre . . . it had all been a part of the only life she had ever known, and now it was no longer necessary. It had all been swept away by an uncalculated accident three months ago, and what was left was—emptiness.

To direct her thoughts away from the maudlin turn they were taking, Lauren helped herself to more bacon and eggs than she could possibly eat and enquired, 'Where's your illustrious house guest this morning?'

Van grinned at her. 'Sitting right across the table from me making a pig of herself.'

She made a face at him and specified, 'I mean, the great Mr Holt.' It occurred to her that he might have already gone home—he had said he wouldn't be staying much longer—and she was not certain why, after the events of last evening, she should find that possibility somewhat disturbing.

Marie answered, 'Oh, he's probably out walking already this morning. He more or less comes and goes as he pleases, and pretty much takes care of himself. He'll probably make his own breakfast later.'

Van buttered a piece of toast and asked casually, not looking at her, 'So what did you think of him, anyway?'

Lauren hesitated for no more than a moment. With anyone other than Van she might have hedged politely, but she saw no point in lying to Van, who knew both her and Shane Holt well enough to guess what her reaction had been. Besides, she sensed more than a casual interest to the question, and she gave him more than a flip answer. 'I thought he was rude, arrogant, conceited, and pompous,' she replied quietly. 'I don't think I've ever been quite so disappointed in anyone in my entire life. I almost wish I hadn't met him at all.'

A brief look passed between Marie and Van, but it was Marie who spoke. 'Shane can be—rather difficult to get to know,' she admitted, and there was a slight reticence in her voice.

'Difficult,' agreed Lauren. 'That's one adjective I left out. Honestly, Marie,' she added seriously, 'I've never met a more unpleasant person. How can you stand to have him around?' She turned to Van. 'Why do you keep inviting him?'

Van smiled ruefully. 'I can tell he went out of his way to put his worst foot forward.' He glanced meaningfully at his wife. 'I was afraid of as much.'

Marie shook her head with a gentle smile. 'I'm afraid you've gotten a bad first impression, Lauren. I'll admit he can be a perfect beast when he wants to be, but, fortunately, that's not most of the time. Actually, he's very nice—basically. You just have to get to know him.'

Lauren finished her cinnamon roll slowly, and took a sip of orange juice. 'I don't mind that so much,' she said in a moment, thoughtfully. 'His being rude and pompous, and even the ego I can understand, I suppose . . .' She gave a slight, self-deprecating smile and admitted, 'I mean, I guess I haven't exactly been an Albert Schweitzer lately myself, but . . .' She glanced down, toying with her napkin, all of the disturbance of the evening before coming back to haunt her in Marie's rosy kitchen. 'It's his attitude towards music that bothers me—hurts me, I suppose is the right word.' She looked at Van, knowing he would understand. 'You know how I've always felt about his music. I never would have believed that he would turn out to be this way. And I can't excuse him for just—*abandoning* it like he did.' She thought of her own lost career and the old anger began to surface. 'He doesn't even care! There *is* no excuse for that.'

Another look filled with silent meaning passed between husband and wife. Lauren was for the first time aware of some sort of secret between the two of them, and she waited expectedly while they decided whether or not to trust her with it. Then Marie touched her napkin to her lips and said quietly, 'There are extenuating circumstances, Lauren. Shane has had a rough time of it.'

'He lost his wife and three-month-old daughter in an

automobile accident,' said Van, 'shortly after his last album was released. He took it very hard.'

Lauren sank back, her anger and her disappointment in the destruction of a legend draining away into simple shock with the one word, 'Oh.' The very phrase 'automobile accident' brought back the horror of her parents' death, and her heart suddenly went out to Shane in empathy and understanding. To lose parents was terrible, and Lauren knew there would always be a special sorrow reserved for them, but it was expected, at some point in everyone's life, eventually. The premature loss of a wife and a baby . . . a dark ache built inside her for a pain she could only imagine.

And then she looked at Van. 'I didn't even know he was married,' she said softly.

Van turned reluctantly back to his breakfast. A pall seemed to have fallen over the table and Lauren had completely lost her elusive appetite. 'He was only married two years—not quite that, actually. He always kept his private life to himself.'

Suddenly Shane Holt was a three-dimensional character to her again, and she wanted to know more. 'How did you meet him?' she asked curiously. 'You never produced any of his records, did you? What's the connection?'

'We got to know one another while I was in Hollywood . . . you remember, it was years ago . . . I was doing the *Aquarius Rising* album.' He smiled a little to himself. 'Now, that dates me, doesn't it?' Then he went on, 'Anyway, we got to know each other—of course, Shane was locked into contracts with another studio, so we never worked together, but we kept up.'

'You never mentioned it to me,' Lauren wondered. 'All this time . . .'

He smiled. 'Discretion is a very valuable asset in this business. Anyway, honey, when we were together we hardly ever had time to talk about business, if you'll recall . . .' He went on with his story. 'After the accident, the press was hounding Shane to no end—I mean really ruthless, and I could see there was no way he was going to be able to handle that. He needed a quiet place to stay with guaranteed privacy ...' He shrugged. 'So he came here. I guess he still looks on the place as a sort of refuge, and, believe it or not, we do enjoy having him. He's not usually the way he was last night, any more than you,' he added meaningfully, 'are usually the way you've been acting lately. Don't judge him too harshly.'

Lauren finished her juice and coffee, and at Marie's insistence, automatically forced down a good portion of her breakfast, but her thoughts were with Shane. She could not get over the fact that the man she had adored in fantasy for so many years had all this time been as close as her best friend ... but it was so typical of Van to take another orphan under his wing, just as he had taken her. And she was glad Van had told her about Shane's past. It made his present behaviour a little easier to understand—not to accept, but to understand—and she did not feel quite so bitter towards him any more.

She asked Marie if there was anything she could do with the housework, but Marie insisted she needed no assistance. 'Everything is automated around here,' she explained brightly. 'I'm just going to put the dishes in the machine and the laundry in the machine, and who needs help with that? Why don't you just wander around and explore the house; make yourself at home.'

Van had gone upstairs to make a business call, so Lauren was left on her own to do exactly that. She had been too tired yesterday to take much of a tour, and she was anxious to see more of the house of which Van was so proud.

It was much too large for two people, Marie had often complained, with five bedrooms, a music room and a spacious rec room, but the extra space did come in handy for the enormous amount of entertaining they did. Lauren knew that it was not unusual for Van to have a houseful of weekend guests, and he often had business associates from Europe and other countries stay for weeks at a time. His outgoing nature and easy hospitality made such invitations always welcome, and Marie thrived on the constant exposure to new and interesting people.

The rec room was just adjacent to the living room, and it contained a pool table, folding tennis table, a projection television and every variety of home video game yet invented. Beyond it, and behind the staircase, was another door which Lauren opened cautiously and quickly closed again. Obviously, it was Shane's room, for the closet door was open and a pair of men's jeans were draped casually over a chair. That explained why they had not bumped into one another yesterday before the party—when he sought isolation, he apparently carried it so far as to seclude himself from other members of the household. Lauren thought that was rather presumptuous of him, considering the fact that there were three other perfectly good unused bedrooms upstairs, and it would surely be easier for Marie to have all her guests occupying the same floor. But she remembered what Marie had said about not judging him too harshly and decided it was really none of her business.

The music room was exactly what she would have expected from Van. It contained a grand piano, an assortment of guitars, several keyboards of some sort, including an electronic synthesiser, and a complicated assortment of recording and play-back equipment. The walls were lined with shelves of records and tapes just like a library, and Lauren was thrilled at the endless possibilities for entertainment they offered. She went over and examined the rows, thinking that he must have a copy of every recording ever made, eager to discover and explore the new vistas of music which had just opened up to her. It did not take her long to determine that the rows were alphabetised, however, and in only a matter of seconds her fingers—almost without her conscious will—were resting on a Shane Holt recording.

The album she withdrew was entitled *Dancers*, and if she had to choose a favourite, she supposed that would be it. She had naturally made a personal identification with the title he had chosen, but the theme of the album went much deeper than that. Throughout the recording he spoke of life as an intricately choreographed dance, and of the harmony between the performers and the music as sometimes frantic, sometimes lilting, sometimes despairing, but always constant. Each song subtly reinforced that theme, often in ways so oblique that only the careful listener could discern the connection, and Lauren supposed one reason she loved it so was because it seemed to hold a secret only she could know . . . which was, of course, the genius behind any creative work.

She was afraid to try to use any of the complicated equipment in the music room, so she took the album into the living room, where a more conventional stereo was placed. As she put the record on the spindle and waited for the first strains of a haunting melody she knew so well, she examined the album cover. It was one of his first, before the time when competition for design awards had become as hot as the competition for Grammies, and it featured simply a full-face photograph of him against a grey background. She still found it hard to believe this could be the same man. Of course the picture had been taken when he was in his mid-twenties, and the long blond hair and the beard were an effective disguise, but this young man, with the smooth, untroubled face and faraway look in his eyes, bore no resemblance whatsoever to the hard, insensitive man she had met last night.

The music began, and Lauren curled up on the sofa, the album cover in her hands, thinking about him. Somehow she had expected the effect of his music to diminish now that she knew the man, but strangely, it had exactly the opposite effect. The opening passages had never thrilled her more, and the following songs moved her to new depths of fascination. The song at the end of the first side told in simple language and clear melody the story of two lovers saying goodbye at a party, and the contrast of the gay party which went on around them and the poignancy of their acceptance of the emptiness which had crept into their lives was so beautiful it brought tears to her eyes.

The only warning she had of a presence behind her was a rush of air and an angry movement, and before she had even drawn a shocked breath the needle arm was jerked from the record with a sharp scratching sound. She jumped to her feet, horror and indignation blotting out the surprise of seeing him, and cried, 'What are you doing? You can't——'

But without even acknowledging her protest, Shane pulled the disc off the spindle and deliberately broke it in half, then hurled the pieces across the room. His face was dark and his lips were white, and when he turned on her the furious turmoil in his eyes caused her to automatically shrink back. For a moment she could only stare at him in horrified disbelief, and when she found her voice it was only a gasp. 'How—dare you! Look what you've done to Van's stereo! You—you broke his record! You had no *right*——'

'No,' he spat back viciously, '*you* had no right!' A dark vein pulsed in his throat and his eyes churned with fury. Lauren had never seen anyone so angry, and it frightened her. 'What the *hell* do you think you're doing?'

'*I* . . .?' Her voice sounded very weak and breathless following his thunderous shout, and incredulity rendered her almost speechless. '*I* was just sitting here minding my own business—you—*you* are the one who came in here acting like a madman! How *dare* you! You're not just mean and arrogant—you're crazy!'

The heated voices had attracted Marie; Lauren could hear her anxious footsteps on the stairs. Apparently Shane noticed them too, because his voice lowered a fraction, even as his fists clenched at his sides and his eyes glittered dangerously. Lauren had never seen such hatred in anyone's eyes—she would never have believed it was possible from him. 'You've been here less than twenty-four hours,' he said lowly, 'and already I'm sick of the sight of you. What in heaven's name was Van thinking of, bringing a star-struck teenager in here——'

'Star-struck!' Lauren laughed wildly even as her eyes stung with angry tears. 'That's the last thing I am! How could anyone be star-struck over a worthless hasbeen, a—an——' she struggled over the words and was surprised that anger made them come only more clearly, 'introverted Quasimodo!'

For a moment Shane looked startled, but swiftly the rage was back again. 'You're an interfering little brat,' he growled, and turned sharply, almost bumping into Marie, who had appeared at the door with alarm and concern stamped on her face. 'Stay the hell out of my life!' he shot over his shoulder, and brushed past Marie without another glance.

'Good heavens!' exclaimed Marie softly, her eyes wide with alarm. 'What was that all about?'

Lauren gulped on an impotent sound of rage and embarrassment, and when she brought her hand to her neck in agitation she was surprised to notice it was shaking. 'That man is—is crazy!' was all she could manage at last, and then Marie noticed the broken record on the floor and she understood.

She went over slowly to pick up the pieces, then began quietly, 'Lauren . . .'

'No,' Lauren said sharply, her eyes flashing, 'I don't want to hear any more excuses for him. He may be your darling and he may have all sorts of problems, but that does not give him the right to act like an animal to people he doesn't even know! This isn't even his house, for Pete's sake, he's a guest here just like I am, but he orders me around like—like something lower than a servant! I honestly don't know why you put up with it, Marie, but I'm warning you, I'm not going to!' And she stalked out of the room and up the stairs.

She should not have attempted such a rash and

dramatic exit; she had not the strength or the co-ordination for it. On the third step she tripped and barely caught herself against the rail before falling. She sat down hard, swearing softly to herself, rubbing her injured knee.

She was not really hurt, but the incident only reminded her that she was clumsy and awkward and she must have looked like a scarlet-faced shrew shouting at Shane Holt a moment ago, and it was as good an excuse as any to let the angry tears come. And that was how Van found her only a few moments later.

He sat down casually beside her and asked, 'Was that the beginning of World War Three I heard, or did the roof merely cave in?'

Lauren sniffed and impatiently rubbed away a tear with the heel of her hand. 'It was that impossible friend of yours! I tell you, Van, the man is——'

'Spare me the gory details.' He lifted his hand mildly. 'I knew it was coming when I heard you playing *Dancers*. I should have warned you, I guess.'

'No, you shouldn't!' she retorted righteously. 'I have a right to play it if I want, and it's not my fault or yours that he can't take being reminded of his failure.' She heard a high-powered engine burst into life, and glanced out the window just in time to see a low red car streak past. 'Good,' she muttered spitefully. 'I hope he stays away. Because if he stays here much longer, I certainly won't!'

She was aware of Van's silence, and she suddenly realized what she had said and how it had sounded. She had repaid Van's kindness and hospitality with a childishness which was no better than Shane Holt's, and she was chagrined. She couldn't look at Van's face and see the hurt and disappointment there, she was too ashamed to have him look at her, so she dropped her head, rubbing her knee absently, not knowing what to say.

Van enquired in a moment, 'Does your knee hurt?'

'It always hurts,' she muttered, still unable to look at him and despising herself.

He dropped a hand lightly on her shoulder as he stood. 'Try to remember,' he advised gently, 'that Shane is always hurting too.'

Lauren tried to make up for her ungracious behaviour by helping Marie prepare lunch and then actually pretending to enjoy it. Shane did not put in an appearance, and Lauren was glad. She didn't think she could take another encounter with him today.

After lunch she went to her room, promising to come down later and help with dinner. But she felt drained, exhausted. She undressed and slipped beneath the coverlet. She remembered nothing else until a dim, far-away pounding stirred the heavy veil of dreamless slumber.

She was aware that the knocking had been going on for some time, but she ignored it. Then she heard a voice—not Van's—impatiently call, 'There's no use pretending you're not in there. You can hear me!'

She turned over slowly in the grey darkness and her eyes focused on the luminous numbers of the digital clock. Seven-fourteen. She had slept for almost four hours!

She sat up abruptly, bringing her hands to her tousled hair and giving herself a little shake to clear the cobwebs of sleep. Four hours! She had never slept that long before in the afternoon, and it seemed as though she had hardly closed her eyes.

And then the voice came again, a little more acerbically this time, and she realised in alarm that it was Shane Holt who addressed her from the other side of the door. 'If you're waiting for an apology you can damn well sit in there and rot! I'm not particularly thrilled at the idea of dining across the table from you, either!'

Lauren slid out of bed and hurried to her closet for a robe, fully awake now and indignant at the thought that he was under the impression he had intimidated her into hiding in her room. She intended to fling open the door and tell him so, but she could hardly do so with any dignity in her underwear, and she couldn't find a robe.

There was a final series of swift raps, then he spoke again, completely out of patience now. 'Look, I was sent up here to fetch you for dinner, but I could personally care less if you starve. Enjoy your sulks; I assure you, I'm going to enjoy my meal.'

She found a robe and drew it on, hurrying to the door with angry words of defence on her lips. But she was too late; Shane was gone.

She dressed in record time, ran a brush through her hair, and descended the stairs with the flush of sleep still on her face and the light of battle in her eyes. The three of them were at the dining room table, just beginning their meal. Van and Marie looked relieved to see her; Shane did not even glance up.

'I'm sorry if I kept you waiting,' she said, looking deliberately at Shane. He chose not to return her glance. 'I was asleep.'

Van looked surprised, and commented, 'Too much sleep during the day isn't good for you.'

And Marie said, as Lauren slipped into her place at the table, 'We wouldn't have disturbed you, dear, but I thought you might be . . .' She broke off delicately, and Lauren realised in amazement that Marie, too, had thought she was simply being sullen by refusing to come to dinner. Well, she told herself uncomfortably, the way she had been behaving lately, what else could she expect them to think? Then Marie added simply, 'At any rate, you can't afford to miss any meals can you? I'm glad you decided to come down.'

And then Lauren felt Shane's eyes upon her, and she went pink with embarrassment. In her hurry, she had pulled on a scoop-necked, much-too-revealing sweater— especially considering the fact that she had nothing to reveal—and a pair of jeans that had fit her last year. Irrationally, she knew she would not have been nearly as bothered by anyone else's seeing her like this, but it had to be Shane Holt. She had never before been so sensitive about her appearance, and once again she was frustrated with herself. It was only one more thing she did not seem to be able to understand about herself lately.

She concentrated on serving her plate generously and eating mechanically, not really tasting anything, while the table conversation went on around her. To her surprise, Shane was quite pleasant to Marie and Van, and did not let the conversation lag. He totally ignored Lauren, which, at that moment, suited her fine. They talked about generalities, local news, the weather forecast, and business, and gradually Lauren began to realise that Shane had more than just an historical interest in Van's talk about business. And then Van said, 'You remember I mentioned to you that new singer I heard about—Jimmy Wild? Well, I had a chance to look him over a few weeks back and I'd like you to meet him.'

Shane glanced up. 'Why don't you handle him yourself?'

'Way out of my league,' replied Van. 'I tell you, this young man could really be something special with the right producer——'

Lauren interrupted, without meaning to, staring at Shane, 'Are you producing now?'

His eyes met hers, one corner of his lips dropped dryly. 'What better occupation for a worthless hasbeen?' he replied politely.

She felt her cheeks go hot and she dropped her eyes quickly. The silence round the table was electric, but, fortunately, it was brief. Lauren was miserable with embarrassment and she busily began to cut her meat, knowing if she tried to eat another bite she would surely choke. She did not know whether to be angry with herself or with Shane, but it was much easier to blame him.

Shane picked up the conversation easily. 'Why don't you have him send me a demo tape?'

Van shook his head. 'No, you've really got to meet

this fellow. Let me call him and see when he can get away.'

Shane lifted an eyebrow. 'That booked, is he?'

'At two-bit dives for a minimum wage,' laughed Van. 'But still, it's a living for him and he's a little bit scared about taking the plunge into the big time . . . especially when we're not promising anything. Let me bring him out; take the time to see what he's got.'

'We'll see,' agreed Shane noncommittally. 'I've got to be getting back pretty soon, though.'

Good, thought Lauren grimly. The sooner the better.

Lauren helped Marie clear the table, discreetly hiding her unfinished portions beneath her napkin, and Van invited Shane to play a game of table tennis. 'Come on, Lauren,' he insisted, 'you can play the winner.'

She shook her head firmly, not looking at either of them. She could feel Shane's eyes on her, waiting for her answer. 'No, thanks, I'm going to wash my hair and then . . .' She almost said 'listen to some records', but she stopped herself just in time. She wasn't even allowed that small comfort any more! She added lamely, 'Go to bed early, I guess. I don't know why I'm so tired—must be the country air.'

Marie took the last of the dishes from Lauren's hands into the kitchen, and Van followed her with the remainder of the unfinished casserole, saying, 'Okay, honey, looks like you're elected. It's no fun unless there's a challenger waiting in the wings . . .'

Lauren was left alone with Shane in the dining room. She glanced at him briefly, and was surprised to find him watching her steadily, a look of thoughtful speculation in his eyes. She quickly avoided his gaze and moved past him towards the stairs.

His voice was soft behind her. 'One question, if I may.'

She stopped, tensing herself for battle, and turned slowly to face him. He would not get the best of her this time. She could give as well as she could take, as soon he would discover—if he had not already.

But his expression was enigmatic. 'What,' he asked simply, 'is an "introverted Quasimodo"? '

Lauren refused to blush; she refused to be embarrassed or intimidated. 'Quasimodo,' she told him evenly, 'was a physical monster, twisted and ugly on the outside, but beautiful on the inside. You,' she informed him without flinching, 'are exactly the opposite.'

For a moment there was utter silence. Nothing changed on his face, there was no hint of expression in his eyes, but she felt something change within the atmosphere. Then he dropped his eyes. 'I see,' he said softly, and turned and left the room.

CHAPTER THREE

To Lauren's surprise, Shane was actually present at breakfast the next morning. She had thought he would make every effort to avoid her for the remainder of his stay, but obviously she had underestimated him—as well as her powers of intimidation. That was a most peculiar meal. Lauren made a concentrated effort to keep up a stream of bright, pleasant conversation with Marie, while Shane did the same with Van, each of them totally ignoring the other while engaging in subtle competition for their hosts' attention. Midway through the meal, Lauren was suddenly struck by how silly it all was and was almost overtaken by a fit of giggles. To her very great surprise, she happened to glance in Shane's direction just then and saw a spark of amusement reflected in his own eyes. She was so taken aback that she forgot what she had been about to say, and broke off in mid-sentence, hastily taking a sip of coffee to cover. All right, Mr Holt, she conceded silently, although without much rancour, first round to you!

After such a stimulating start to the day, Lauren found herself in surprisingly good spirits, and she insisted upon helping Marie with the housework. This time, perhaps sensing Lauren's restlessness, Marie offered no protests, and dispatched her guest with a basket of furniture polish and dust-cloths to make the rounds of the house. It was busy work and Lauren knew it, for Marie was such an assiduous housekeeper she did not allow so much as a speck of dust or a smudge to appear on her furniture during the day before polishing it away, but Lauren enjoyed the illusion of feeling useful again and had no urge to complain.

There was a moment when she felt slightly

40

uncomfortable upon entering the music room and
remembering how her own foolish sentiment had got
her into trouble yesterday. But she quickly shrugged
that aside. She had a right to be here if she wanted, and
besides, now she was curious about something else. So
the great Shane Holt was now lending his inestimable
talent to the production side of music. She wondered
which of these recordings had his name on the label,
which artists he sponsored, and if any of them were
any good.

She soon realised that discovering the answers to
those questions would be an impossible task, unless she
wanted to manually go through every one of the
thousand-odd records Van had in his collection. She
could always ask Van, of course, but she told herself
that she really wasn't that interested, and there was too
much of a possibility that Shane might discover her
curiosity and demand to know the reason for it. She
was quite convinced by now that the less the two of
them saw of each other the better off they both would
be.

Still, as she dusted, she could not prevent her fingers
from trailing absently over the covers, and soon she
found her attention again upon the small Shane Holt
collection. And there was a surprise. The copy of
Dancers that he had destroyed yesterday had been
replaced, and she drew it out thoughtfully, noticing that
it was a brand new copy; not even the price tag or the
cellophane wrap had been removed. She knew Marie
had not purchased it yesterday, and she doubted that
Van had made a special trip, so that left only . . .

She heard a footfall behind her and whirled guiltily,
the incriminating album still clutched in her hands.

'Relax,' Shane said lazily, raising both hands in a
gesture of peace. 'I'm unarmed.'

She turned quickly and replaced the record, then
blurted, 'Did you replace this?'

His smile was dry and humourless. 'I always pay for
my mistakes,' he answered simply.

She noticed he had pulled on a light plaid wool jacket over the denim shirt and jeans he had worn at breakfast, and changed into hiking boots. He looked at home in such an outfit, just as he looked at home in Van's house among the mountains—rugged, outdoorsy, and very masculine. Then he said abruptly, 'I'm going for a walk in the hills. Do you want to come?'

Lauren almost dropped the basket of cleaning supplies as she lifted it from the desk, and her reply was automatic and startled. 'No!'

His next question took her off guard even more. 'Why not?'

She turned to him, her eyes wide with astonishment. 'I should think that would be fairly obvious.'

But he ignored the obvious and said, 'I understand you recently underwent orthopaedic surgery. Didn't your surgeon advise you of the beneficial effects of walking to strengthen your muscles and improve your overall general health?'

She simply stared at him. She had a very strong feeling he was simply laying a nasty trap for her, for why would he invite her company when he had already made it clear he could not stand her presence? But she only said irritably, 'You talk like a college professor!'

'Why does that surprise you?' He came over to her easily, removing the basket from her hands and replacing it on the desk. 'You know so much about me; you should also know I was a college professor before I was a musician.'

'No,' she said uncomfortably. 'I didn't know that.'

'One year of elucidating the virtues of T.S. Eliot and John Steinbeck to a group of adolescents who were more concerned with how to get into the best fraternity than the meaning of life was enough for me. I thought there surely must be an easier way to make a living, so . . .' he shrugged, delivering it like a challenge, 'the rest is history.'

But Lauren refused to be drawn into another scene.

She started to step away from him, saying, 'If you'll excuse me, I have to——'

His hand closed firmly about her forearm. 'No,' he repeated her words back to her from the night of the party, 'I will not excuse you. Marie says you're very delicate and must be treated with the utmost care, and that we should all do our part to see you back to health. And heaven knows, I always do my part. So you'll walk with me.'

She glared at him, resenting Marie for making her an object of solicitation and Shane for so glibly taking advantage of it. She tried to pull her arm away, replying coolly, 'I'm touched by your concern, but I assure you——'

He refused to let her go. 'Look,' he said impatiently, 'we can stand here all day and argue about it or you can come with me now and get the worst over with. I don't know about you, but Van and Marie happen to be very important to me and I refuse to make their home a battleground.'

'Ha!' she exclaimed, pulling at her arm again. 'Look who's talking! Mr Diplomacy himself!'

Now there was actually a spark of amusement in his eye. 'If you could see how ridiculous you look, struggling with a man twice your size over a simple thing like a walk, I'm sure you would be more reasonable.'

She dropped her eyes obstinately to the grip he still had on her arm, and she knew he was right. And it was just barely possible that he was making a genuine overture towards peace for the sake of their hosts, and the least she could do was meet him half way. 'All right,' she agreed at last, rather uncharitably. 'But let me go.'

Shane released her arm and politely gestured her ahead of him towards the door.

He showed her to a path which curved around the back of the house towards the mountains, partially through open fields, partially through shadowed wood.

Like yesterday, this day was clear and beautiful. The air was cool and fresh, the sky was a rich, deep, almost surrealistic blue, and the way the morning sun reflected off the mountains made them look more than three-dimensional. The air was sweet with the fragrance of pine and spruce and the chirping of the birds melodious, and Lauren wished she could relax and enjoy the walk. But she was too aware of his presence, too concerned over his sudden change of attitude towards her, and too busy trying to arm herself for the inevitable battle she could sense coming. She knew that he was checking his own long stride to keep up with her limping gait, and that made her uncomfortable. It seemed as though just being around him made the limp worse, and she wished she had never allowed him to talk her into this.

Coming out of the short stretch of wood, the terrain became steeper and rockier. Lauren was becoming tired—she had not realised she was so out of shape—and more than once she turned her foot on a loose stone which had spilled from the mountain base. On the last occasion she very nearly fell, and only his strong grip on her arm saved her.

'You should get some good hiking shoes,' he commented, looking down at her moccasined feet. 'You're going to kill yourself in those things, or at the very least, break your ankle.'

'Thanks,' she replied, trying not to pant for breath as the climb grew more arduous, 'but I don't intend to do anything this stupid again, so I don't think they would be worth the investment.'

'You should do it every day,' he replied, guiding her around another spray of shattered boulders which blocked the path. 'That is, unless you want to go through the rest of your life with that unsightly limp.'

Lauren jerked her arm away, demanding gruffly, 'What do you know about it?'

'I've had a few ski injuries,' Shane responded mildly. 'Nothing as bad as yours, of course, but enough to give me the basics of physical therapy, and to know,' he added, slipping his arm about her waist, 'that your knee is probably killing you right about now. Let's rest over here.'

She had no intention of arguing with him over that, and he led her to a small grassy knoll sprinkled with small blue wildflowers and feathery pine-cones. He brushed away the pine-cones and then, with surprising thoughtfulness, offered his hands for balance as she clumsily lowered herself to the ground. This unexpected attention made her uncomfortable, and the feel of his strong, steady hands beneath her fingers—just as his arm about her waist had a moment ago—made her feel shy and gangly and much too aware of him as a physical being, rather than just an object for anger or spite.

Shane stretched out on the grass beside her, very close, his long legs crossed at the ankles, leaning back on his elbows. The wind ruffled his hair, and she noticed that its pale brown colour was peppered with just the faintest hint of silvery grey—something noticeable only in bright sunlight, she supposed—and that his features, when not gathered into a stormy frown or distorted by sarcasm, were quite pleasant to look at. Now the sun shadowed his face interestingly, emphasising the healthy brown of his skin and the tiny crinkles about his mouth and his eyes, and reflecting a clear, untroubled light in the multi-coloured depths of his eyes. Before meeting him, Lauren had never before thought of him as attractive—she hadn't thought he was unattractive; she simply hadn't thought of it at all—and it came as something of a surprise to her to notice that he was very well built, with strong shoulders and arms, firmly muscled thighs which were clearly defined by the tight jeans he wore, flat abdomen and broad chest which he showed to advantage with tailored shirts. the contrast between his healthy masculinity and her own lack of feminine attributes was painfully apparent to Lauren; it made her wish she had worn a bulky coat to hide her thin chest and skinny hips, that she had taken time to put on a little make-up this morning or at least checked her hair in the mirror before they left. It made her feel ridiculously like an awkward thirteen-year-old, and that was an image which particularly grated, because he had already made it clear that was exactly how he saw her.

She turned her eyes away from him and tried to concentrate on the view, which was, in fact, spectacular. The valley stretched below them in all its vibrant shades of red and gold, the blue-green of a mountain rose to the west, and, by straining her eyes, she could just make out a hazy strip of highway in the distance. Directly below them was a glimpse of the roof of the house, and she was surprised they had come this far. She encircled her knee with her arms and sighed, 'My, this is pretty, isn't it?'

'Hmm.' He plucked up a tiny blue flower and absently tossed it aside. 'All it needs is big black letters in the sky saying "Come to Colorado". Picture-postcard perfect.'

Lauren glanced at him suspiciously, wondering if he was retreating into his familiar cynicism, but there was no sign of it on his face. She tried to keep the conversation neutral. 'When are you leaving?'

'A few days,' he responded, his eyes upon the distant landscape. 'I like to be back on the coast before the snow starts to fly.' And then he glanced at her. 'It can't be any too soon for you, I imagine.'

She replied evenly, proud of her composure, 'I don't know why you say that. It doesn't make any difference to me what your plans are.'

'Oh, no?' He shifted his gaze back to the horizon. 'It's obvious you've been fretting since you got here, and you resent the fact that Van and Marie aren't giving you their undivided attention. You counted on having them petting and pampering you all winter, didn't you? You have to be centre stage and you don't like sharing the spotlight.'

She gaped at him. 'That's—ridiculous!' She was genuinely incensed. 'I never did or said anything to give you that impression—how dare you make such a rash judgment! What I—*resent* is your high-handed manner and overbearing methods, not to mention your uncontrollable temper and your damned arrogance! And if you want to know the truth, no, you can't leave any too soon for me. Things will be a lot more pleasant around here when you do!'

'Ah, well,' he said negligently, and she knew he had been baiting her. 'What can you expect from a person who's twisted and ugly on the inside?' He glanced at her. 'A spiritual and emotional monster, I believe you said?'

'Implied,' she corrected coldly, even though her cheeks were burning with that ruthless reminder of her heartless treatment of him yesterday.

Shane remained completely unruffled. 'So,' he said, plucking up another flower and carelessly tossing it aside, 'if you didn't come here to be adored and catered to, what are you doing here?'

'What do you mean?' she replied huffily. 'I was invited.'

'You didn't have anything better to do than live off the charity of friends for the winter?'

Her eyes darkened, and with a great effort she controlled her temper. She said simply, 'No.'

'Why aren't you working?'

'Look,' she said evenly, proud of the way she was refusing to lose control no matter how he goaded her, 'if you know about my injury, you also know that I was a dancer. I can't do that any more. That's why I'm here, and that's why I'm not working.'

'I see,' he reflected, carefully pulling the petals one by one off another wildflower. 'In other words, you're a worthless hasbeen.'

She caught her breath, amazed at how easily and neatly she had stepped into his trap. She fought the impulse to rage at him, or to simply get up and stalk away, for it was much more satisfying to give him back his own. 'Oh,' she said softly, and with deceptive mildness, 'very clever. Of course you overlooked one minor detail. I was forced to give up my career. You *chose* to give up yours.'

He turned to look at her, leaning on one elbow, and the swift anger she had expected her comment to provoke was noticeably absent in his expression. 'I merely wanted to make a point,' he said. 'I don't think either one of us wants to engage in mortal combat with the other—besides the fact that it's embarrassing Marie and Van and putting a lot of unneccessary stress on all our nerves, it's a waste of time and energy. There's no reason we can't behave like civilised people and even get along fairly well together as long as we keep to one simple rule: you stay out of my business and I'll stay out of yours.'

'I assure you I have no interest in your business whatsoever,' she told him coolly, but she could not resist one final stab. 'Especially since you don't have any business any more to be interested in.'

Shane muttered an oath and rolled over on his back, his splayed fingers across his forehead shielding his eyes from the sun. 'This is marvellous,' he said dryly. 'I may as well go home now; I can see I'm going to have you like an albatross around my neck until I do.' She bristled, but he went on, 'Do you realise, Miss Davis, that I've managed my life quite well for the past thirty-three years without any help whatsoever from star-struck adolescents . . .'

She interrupted him firmly, and with great self-control, 'If you brought me all the way up here just to insult me or to pick a fight, you could have saved yourself the trouble and done it just as well at home. And as a matter of fact, that's just where I'd like to be right now.'

She started to rise, but his hand lightly on her arm stopped her. As he looked at her his expression changed from mild annoyance to something less readable, and he said thoughtfully, 'No, I don't think I brought you here to insult you. Or maybe I did. Maybe I thought it was about time I evened the score.' His eyes were very clear, the tone of his voice serious. She was acutely aware of the light touch of his fingers on her arm and she could not make herself pull away. 'Maybe,' he continued, 'I thought I could spare Marie's and Van's ears by fighting with you up here, or maybe I really thought it was possible for us to make peace. Or maybe . . .' His hand trailed from her arm to her waist, his fingers warm and sure against the fragile outline of her ribs. His voice softened a fraction, and his face suddenly seemed much closer. '. . . I brought you here just to do this . . .'

Lauren's heart lurched and quickened and a thousand things streaked through her mind in that half second as his fingers tightened imperceptibly on her waist and his face moved closer to hers. There was a leaping of pulses and an incredible difficulty breathing as the reality of the unexpected moment leapt upon her—the moment she had yearned for in dreams so secret she would not even admit them to herself, the time when she would be wrapped in Shane Holt's embrace and feel his lips upon hers. There was the overpowering need to slip her arms about him and draw him close and let herself be totally lost to that one ecstatic moment of fantasy . . . There was the warmth of his breath on her cheek, the lazy intent in his eyes, the touch of his fingers on her ribs and the overwhelming nearness of him . . . Acutely aware of his vital masculinity and her own frail incompetence, she turned her face away abruptly.

'Let's go,' she said quickly, and got to her feet.

She started down the hill at a clumsy, uneven pace, and did not look back. After a moment she heard Shane get up and follow her.

For a time he walked behind her, and she used the solitude to regain her composure, to make an effort to cool her cheeks and steady her breathing. She was frustrated with herself and with him, and she still felt shaky inside, very aware of the limp which had intensified with physical fatigue and emotional stress. She felt clumsy and ungainly, homely and unattractive, and angry with him for making her so aware of it.

After a time he lengthened his stride and walked beside her, his hands in his pockets, his demeanour casual. And then he asked mildly, 'Is there something I should know about what just happened up there?'

She swallowed hard on her embarrassment. He did not even have the grace to let it drop. What should she expect? She could hedge, or ignore his question, or try to outwalk him and probably end up breaking her neck. She stopped and turned to him defiantly, and responded, 'I'm just getting a little tired of being mocked, and I think you have a pretty perverted sense of humour.'

His eyes reflected genuine astonishment. 'There's something perverted about wanting to kiss a pretty girl? I would think it would be perverted if I *didn't* try. I happen to find you attractive——'

'Ha!' She turned on her heel with an angry sound of bitter laughter. 'It must be a long time since you've had a woman, then.'

His startled bark of laughter sent a hot flush to her cheeks and she could have bitten her tongue, only that would not bring the hasty, uncalculated words back. She refused to look at him. 'Why, Miss Davis,' he exclaimed, keeping up with her, 'you do say the crudest things!' She could feel his amused gaze upon her and she avoided it deliberately, quickening her stumbling steps. Then he added casually, 'As a matter of fact, it has been a fairly long time, but what has that to do with anything?'

She turned to him, her cheeks flaming, determined to put an end to this conversation. 'Look,' she said steadily, 'I'm not attractive. I'm skinny and awkward and . . .' she gestured viciously towards her leg, 'crippled. You don't even like me—we both know that. What I don't know is what kind of perverse pleasure you thought you would get out of coming on to me, because it certainly wasn't physical——'

There was an odd, wicked look in his eye which should have warned her as he interrupted mildly, 'Well, I don't know about that; you didn't give me a chance to find out.' And then he drew her to him, full length, before she had time to even draw a breath of protest, catching her so off guard she did not have even a moment to struggle. And then, swiftly, efficiently, pressing her close to his strong thighs and broad chest, he ran his hands over her slight body from hips to waist to shoulders—without intimacy or affection, but deftly and impersonally. Then he pronounced carelessly, 'You're right: all sharp angles and flat planes. Nothing interesting there.'

Lauren hurled herself away from him with a muffled, angry sob; immediately she tripped over a root and almost went sprawling, and then his strong hands were on her waist, drawing her to her feet. She felt insulted and violated, and she hated him. Laughter danced in his eyes and teasing words were on his lips, but one look at her scarlet cheeks and glittering eyes erased his amusement. His expression changed to muted amazement and he said softly, 'Hey, you're really serious!'

She struggled against his hold on her waist. 'Let me go,' she demanded, through clenched teeth. 'Just—let me go!'

For a moment he seemed undecided, then he said, 'And watch you fall down this hill and break both your legs?' he slipped his arm about her waist and took a firm clasp on her left arm with his free hand. 'Lean on me,' he suggested quietly. 'It will be easier that way, and I know you're tired.'

She struggled once more, violently. To her chagrin, she felt her eyes burn with angry tears. 'I don't need your pity!'

'Oh no?' Shane responded mildly, totally oblivious to her ineffectual efforts to free herself. He started walking again and she had no choice but to follow. 'I thought that was exactly what you wanted. Or are you feeling sorry enough for yourself that you don't have room for anyone's else's concern?'

'You're an impossible man!' she choked, and hated the feel of his arm about her and his hand supporting her—in exactly the same way a nurse would assist an invalid patient. 'I wish you'd just leave me alone!'

'I seem to recall making the same request of you not too long ago.'

Lauren took an unsteady breath, and stopped. He allowed her enough freedom of movement to turn and look at him, and she said quietly, 'All right, you've made your point. I'm sorry I interfered in your life and I'll stay out of your way from now on. Fair?'

He answered her evenly, 'And I'm sorry for what I said a minute ago. I didn't realise you were so sensitive about it. I wasn't trying to be cruel.' And then he slipped his arm through hers and started walking again. 'Also, you should know I don't apologise very often, so you have every right to be impressed.'

But Lauren did not feel impressed. She felt abused and drained and victimised by the troubled emotions which were clashing within her. She just didn't want to fight any more.

When they reached the house she went to her room and slept until dinner time.

CHAPTER FOUR

FOR the next few days Lauren did keep strictly out of his way, and Shane regarded her efforts with a sort of amused perplexity. Several times he made overtures of friendliness to her—usually within the sight or hearing of Marie and Van, for the sake of a good impression—but she received them indifferently. Most of the time he wasn't around anyway; he spent his time on endless walks in the mountains or fishing for trout in a nearby stream, or cloistered with Van presumably discussing business. Lauren wandered aimlessly through the long days, resisting Marie's attempts to entertain her, going to bed early and getting up late, and becoming accustomed to long afternoon naps.

One day at lunch Marie expressed concern over Lauren's apparent boredom. Lauren tried to dismiss it politely by commenting, 'It *is* very restful here.' A chuckle went around the table, and then she had to admit, 'But I really don't see what you two find to do with yourselves all winter. How do you keep from going stir-crazy?'

'Well, it's bound to be an adjustment,' Van agreed, 'after the life you've been used to. But we manage to keep occupied. As long as we're not snowed in there's no problem, but when we can't get out of the house we just try to make the best of it. Television, video games, cosy evenings snuggling by the fire . . .' He glanced at his wife with a grin. 'Going to bed early.'

'Well, that's all very fine for you two,' commented Shane as Marie gave her husband a demure look and turned back to her salad, 'but Lauren has no one to snuggle up with, and going to bed early can be pretty boring when you do it alone. Did it ever occur to you, that she might be missing the company of people her own age, or perhaps even be mooning over a lost lover?'

Lauren stared at him, aghast that he would dare mock her so blatantly in the presence of Marie and Van, but there was no sign of mockery on his face—only bland concern. Among his many other talents, she discovered bitterly, he was also a consummate actor. And how dared he patronise her, make a point of embarrassing her . . .

Marie interrupted her furious condemnations to enquire curiously, 'Is that so, Lauren? You never mentioned . . .'

And the worst was, he even had Marie believing it! 'No,' she said shortly, 'I'm perfectly happy here and I don't miss anyone. I'm afraid Shane was just making a rather tasteless joke.'

'It's my perverted sense of humour again,' Shane told her blandly, and then suggested, 'What about that young man you left behind—your partner?'

Again she stared at him. 'Joel? He was just my partner, there was nothing. . .' And then she demanded suspiciously, 'How did you know about him?'

Van looked embarrassed, and Shane shrugged. 'Word gets around.'

Marie quickly changed the subject, and when she and Van were successfully engaged in their own conversation, Lauren demanded of Shane in a furious undertone, 'I thought the deal was we stay out of each other's business.'

He looked innocent. 'I don't recall making any such deal.'

'We made a bargain,' she reiterated, seething. 'I've kept my part of it, and the last thing I expected was for you to go back on yours. You broke your promise!'

'I don't break promises,' he responded mildly, and turned back to his meal, totally unconcerned. 'Mostly because I don't make them.'

She opened her mouth for a scathing retort, but then closed it again. The last thing she wanted was to get into a verbal battle with him at the lunch table with Van and Marie as referees. She missed his look of guarded surprise at his easy victory.

After lunch, she helped Marie with the few dishes, and then wandered up to her room while the others were occupied elsewhere. She picked up a paperback book she had been half heartedly reading the past few days, but she could not get interested in it. She found it hard to concentrate on anything these days. She supposed Van was right, it would take a while to adjust to the sedentary life after having been accustomed to twelve-hour days of rehearsal and conditioning, the frantic travel, the constant excitement and challenge . . . The lights, the applause, the camaraderie of the theatre, the new faces and new places, the constant adrenaline high which was part of life on the road . . . Oh, how she missed it! Even thinking of it now caused a little knot of yearning to form in her stomach and slowly spread with despair throughout her body. She would never adjust to it. Not ever.

She turned over on her stomach and went to sleep.

The next thing she was aware of was hands gripping her shoulders and a muffled voice calling her name far away. It seemed as though she had only just closed her eyes, and she was so tired it was so pleasant to just lie there and dream nothing, she did not want to wake up yet. She mumbled something which was meant to be, 'Go away!' and tried to turn away from the fingers that were digging into her shoulders.

'Lauren!' Shane jerked her to a sitting position, shaking her hard, so hard that her hair tumbled over her face and she could only gasp in alarm and disorientation, fighting him off weakly. 'Wake up, damn you! What's the matter with you?'

'Stop it!' she managed, pushing at her hair with one hand and his shoulder with the other. 'What are you—' She was still too foggy with sleep to be angry, only confused. 'Stop!' she gasped as he shook her once more. 'You're hurting me!'

He released the pressure on her shoulders only slightly, and demanded cautiously, 'Are you awake? What the hell are you doing?'

She simply stared at him dazedly, letting her arms drop to her side and replying stupidly, 'Sleeping.'

A sort of impatient fear darkened his eyes as he glared at her. 'I couldn't wake you up,' he said roughly. 'I thought you might have taken something.' Once again his fingers tightened painfully on her shoulders and he gave her a little shake, demanding, 'Did you?'

'W-what?' She still could not quite make sense of it all. 'You mean—pills? N-no, why should I? Let me go!'

He let her go so abruptly that she fell back against the headboard, and he got up and opened the curtains with two swift, angry jerks. The bright afternoon sun spilled into the room, casting him into shadow and causing Lauren to blink and shield her eyes against its painful glare. 'So this is what you've been doing up here every day!' he exclaimed, and there was an impatience and a thinly checked fury in his tone she simply did not understand. 'I thought you were just trying to avoid me—hell, why stop with me when you can avoid the whole world, right?'

She pushed her hair away from her face with both hands, focusing on him as her eyes adjusted to the light and her mind gradually adjusted to the indignity to which she had just been subjected. 'What are you doing here?' she demanded. 'How dare you come barging into my bedroom and wake me up——'

'It's about time someone did!' He turned abruptly away from her, and the tension and anger radiated from every line of his body. Then, as though forcibly commanding himself to relax, he ran his fingers through his hair and released a soft breath. 'All right,' he said in a moment, in a much calmer tone. 'I'm sorry I was so rough with you. I know I must have scared you, but you've got to understand you gave me a pretty big scare too.'

Her puzzlement overrode her anger for the moment, but before she could say anything he came and sat beside her on the bed. The lines of his face were still tight, but there was a rueful expression in his eye which allowed her to cautiously relax a little. 'Sleep is a convenient escape,' he said, 'but not always a healthy one. Sometimes it's just a sign of cowardice.'

She glowered at him. 'I don't know what you're talking about.' She wanted to get out of bed, and she knew that would be the dignified thing to do. She was still confused and disorientated, and Shane's presence so close to her on the rumpled bed made her uncomfortable—she did not trouble to analyse why, she just knew that it did. But she did not want to jump out of bed with her limbs still feeling so heavy and stiff, only to once again have him witness her clumsiness, so she simply moved away from him, taking a pillow and hugging it to her as though for protection. 'You had no right to come up here and wake me up—but then you're always doing things you had no right to do.'

'I'm glad you noticed,' he responded evenly. 'Now you won't be surprised at anything I do in the future.'

She swallowed hard at that; the implication made her very nervous. But she only said, 'I'm too tired to fight with you. Go away.'

'You're not tired, Lauren,' he answered curtly, 'just lazy.' He plucked the pillow from her hands and tossed it on the floor. 'Get up. We're going into town.'

She was so astounded by his behaviour that she forgot all those indignant protests she might have made and instead blurted only, 'Why?'

'For supplies,' he told her, and, grasping both her hands, pulled her to her feet. 'We're having company, so Marie's too busy to do it.'

She looked at him suspiciously, still pushing at her tangled hair with her fingers, uneasy over the invitation and the casualness with which it was issued. 'What kind of supplies?'

'No one faces a Colorado winter without some preparation,' he answered. 'It's a good idea to have emergency supplies laid in early.'

'Why should you care about winter supplies?' demanded Lauren uncharitably. 'You won't even be here then.'

'Well, it so happens there's been a change of plans.' he searched around and found her shoes on the floor beside the bed. 'And even if there hadn't been, it wouldn't kill me to help Marie out in a pinch. Come on, put these on.' He handed her shoes to her. 'We'll have to leave now if we expect to be back by dark.'

She hesitated, then sat down on the bed to put on her shoes. She wasn't entirely sure she wanted to go with him, but the invitation, and the motive behind it, was too intriguing to refuse. 'What kind of change of plans?' she asked cautiously, tying her laces.

'Van has talked me into hanging around and meeting that new singer. I may be here as late as the middle of October.'

He seemed to be watching her face closely for a reaction, and she was careful not to give him one— despite the fact that, on hearing those words, she felt more awake than she had since he had entered the room, energised and ready for a challenge. Another month with Shane! It appeared her winter was not going to be as restful as she planned, after all.

She went over to the mirror and began to brush her hair into some semblance of neatness, fastening it at the neck with a simple leather clasp. She wished he would leave the room so that she could change into something more attractive than the plain plaid shirt she was wearing over her jeans, which seemed to be too large at the shoulders and much too large in the bust. But she enquired simply, 'So who's the company? When are they arriving?'

'Tonight,' he answered her last question first, watching her in the mirror without much interest. 'Just some record people. Some pretty big names, as a matter of fact. Do you think you can control yourself, or will we have to lock you in your room to keep you from drooling all over the celebrities?'

She whirled on him, restraining a wild impulse to throw the hairbrush at him, swift anger flaming in her cheeks and glittering in her eyes. 'You creep!' she cried. 'It really pains you to be nice, doesn't it? And just when I think you've got the act down pat you go and make some dirty little comment——'

His eyes sparkled with mild amusement. 'I just wanted to see if you were still the same girl I met a week ago. It's been kind of hard to tell, the way you've been moping about lately.' He extended his arm to her. 'Shall we go?'

She was astounded, and still furious. 'What makes you think I would go anywhere with you, you sanctimonious——'

'Fine.' He shrugged lightly, that nasty little gleam of self-assured amusement still in his eyes. 'Rage at me, spit at me, call me every name you know—there's nothing like a little righteous indignation to get the circulation going. But you're also coming into town with me, so let's get going.'

Lauren glared at him, and her meaning was perfectly clear as she responded coldly, 'You're right—I am.' Because she simply would not give him the satisfaction of having cowered her, or allow him another victory in the endless battle of wills. If this was the way he wanted it, fine; he would find he had got more than he bargained for!

She refused his offered arm and stalked past him down the stairs.

They took Van's Scout, and Lauren noticed that Shane was a cautious driver—exhibiting not fear, but respect for the machine he was commanding. She knew that she, too, had become a much more responsible driver after the accident which had taken her parents, and for a moment it was hard to be angry with Shane.

He stopped on the highway for gas, and when he returned from paying the attendant he slid behind the wheel and tossed a candy bar into her lap. She stared at it. 'What's this?'

'Calories,' he responded, starting the ignition. 'Or a peace offering, however you want to look at it.'

She glanced at him, trying to hide her amusement behind an expression of suspicious disapproval. 'You must think I come pretty cheap.'

'Every woman has her price,' he responded, and swung out on to the highway. He reached into his pocket and brought out four more candy bars, then tossed them to her, one by one. 'Name yours.'

She burst into laughter as she caught the last one and scrambled for two more which had fallen on the floor. Shane glanced at her as she straightened up, smiling. 'Do you know,' he said, 'that's the first time I've heard you laugh. Was it really so painful?'

She took up one of the candy bars and looked at it thoughtfully, choosing to ignore his remark. 'It's been years since I had one of these.' She marvelled over how long it had really been—perhaps since she was a child. From the moment she had begun to take her dancing seriously she had resigned herself to a life of grapefruit and cottage cheese, and she had never looked back.

'So live dangerously,' he urged, his eyes upon the road. 'After all, a whole new world is opening up to you now.'

Yes, she thought bleakly, a whole new world . . . But she opened the candy and glanced at him curiously, commenting, 'You're not talking like a college professor any more.'

'I know,' he answered. 'I only do that with people I don't . . .'

He hesitated, and she supplied, 'Know?'

'Like,' he corrected.

Lauren did not know quite how to take that, so she let it drop. As she bit into the rich, chewy chocolate she discovered she felt less and less like arguing with him.

In that short afternoon she discovered a Shane Holt she had never met before. He was not like she had imagined him, and not like she knew him, but somehow a compromise between the two. He was haphazard and careless about the shopping, checking Marie's list only after he had left the store and often returning for things he had forgotten. In the supermarket, he seemed to throw into the cart whatever struck his fancy, and they ended up with four sacks of groceries when Lauren, who had been entrusted with the grocery list, knew for a fact that Marie had requested only twelve items. He escorted Lauren into a sporting goods store and, ignoring her protests, had her fitted for a pair of hiking boots. While he was there, he picked up a Stetson hat with a colourful feather headband that had caught his eye, paid an exorbitant price for it, and only later admitted he would probably never wear it.

'And they say women are bad shoppers!' exclaimed Lauren in exasperation as they stuffed the last of the packages into the back of the Scout. 'Look at all this junk, and only half of it—if that much—has anything at all to do with what Marie asked you to buy.'

He shrugged it off. 'Life is too short to spend all your time labouring over decisions. The thing to do is go with the impulse, and sort out your mistakes later.'

'Like my boots,' she decided, climbing into the passenger seat. 'That's one mistake you can sort out right now, because I'm not going to wear them.'

'Yes, you are,' he told her mildly, and backed out of the parking space. 'Every day you're going to walk until the snow drifts up over your head. That's the only way you're ever going to get back into condition.'

Lauren opened her mouth to demand impertinently why he was showing such a sudden interest in her health and what business it was of his, but she decided against it. The day had been too lovely to spoil now . . . in fact, for the first time in months she felt relaxed and at ease, and she realised in amazement that she had actually enjoyed herself. This must be the Shane Marie and Van knew and loved, she reflected, a man who was easy-going and pleasant, concerned and interested, energetic and stimulating. She only wished he had let her see this part of him earlier, and she wished she had never known the less admirable side of his personality, because now she would always be wondering which part of him was the real Shane Holt—or if it was a mixture of both.

'Van and Marie will probably be gone when we get back,' he told her, driving into the clear pink and green sunset. 'She said we would have to make do for ourselves for dinner, so we may as well eat out. What would you like?'

'Why didn't I know about any of this?' Lauren complained. 'Marie never mentioned company to me, or anything about dinner.'

'If you'd been paying attention to what was going on around you,' he answered, 'you would have known. We discussed it all at breakfast this morning. Van and Marie have to be at the airport at eight o'clock this evening, so what do you want for dinner?'

Vaguely Lauren remembered something of a discussion of that sort, and some controversy about who was to meet the plane. She really hadn't been paying much attention to anything lately. And she wondered why Shane had elected to stay at home and do shopping rather than go with Van, when it was obvious these were people he knew. She was about to ask him when he interrupted her thought with, 'Chinese? Italian? Mexican? It's your choice.'

'Oh.' She decided not to push her luck with too many questions and just enjoy his new, amiable mood. She smiled at him. 'Let's eat American. Hamburgers.'

But, as they took a small table in a corner of one of the fast food restaurants which dotted the highway, Shane turned the tables on her by enquiring, 'What are you going to do with yourself when Van's hospitality wears out at the end of the winter?'

Once again, he was clearly breaking the rules which maintained their respective privacy. She hesitated, wondering what he was up to now, and then she replied cautiously, 'I don't know. I haven't thought about it.'

'Don't you think it's something you should think about?'

She took a sip of the thick vanilla milk shake; it was

very cold and made her shiver. She replied evenly, 'I think it's none of your business.'

'Oh-oh,' he said softly. There was a mischievous twinkle of challenge in his eye which made it much more difficult than usual to be irritated with him. 'Now I've made you mad. And I was trying so hard to be nice!'

'I noticed that,' Lauren responded negligently, taking up her hamburger. 'I've been wondering all day why you're going to so much trouble.'

He appeared to think about that. 'I'm not really sure,' he answered at last. 'I think it might be because I've recently been reminded how much I dislike being called names.'

'You must be used to it,' she answered with a sweet smile, and popped a french fry into her mouth.

'That doesn't mean I like it,' he told her seriously, and somehow the new inflection of frankness in his voice made her more uneasy than any of his teasing or insults had done.

She changed the subject quickly. 'If you like Colorado enough to spend your summers here, why don't you live here?'

'I used to,' he replied. He had finished eating while she picked at her food, pretending an appetite, and now he sat back and sipped his coffee. 'I was raised here as a matter of fact. But I told you, I don't like the snow.'

'You ski,' she reminded him.

Suddenly he dropped his eyes. There was a silence, a change of mood, that completely baffled her. Then he looked at her again, and the expression on his face was no more than thoughtful. 'I can see you and I are going to have a lot of trouble communicating. We both have too many touchy subjects in our lives, and we seem to have an uncanny knack for zeroing in on each other's vulnerabilities.'

Lauren had had no idea that the mention of skiing would be a vulnerable area for him, but then there were so many things—painful associations with his past—

which she had no way of knowing about him. Yet for
the first time he had not reacted to her stumbling upon
these sensitive areas with anger or withdrawal, and she
was a bit taken aback. She did not quite know how to
respond, so she dropped her eyes to her half-finished
hamburger and shrugged, 'A lot of people don't
communicate.'

'They do if they want to get to know each other
better,' he answered.

Her eyes flew to his face in surprise, but he was
perfectly serious. 'Why,' she questioned in astonishment,
so startled she uttered the first words which came to
mind, 'would you want to get to know me better?'

He smiled a little, but his eyes were studious as they
examined her face. 'I've been asking myself that same
question for the past four days,' he answered in a
moment. 'I've decided it must be because you make me
so angry. It's been a long time since anyone was able to
do that to me, believe it or not, and I think that
qualifies you as a person worth knowing.'

Now she really did not know what to say. Was she to
be flattered because he wanted to find out more of what
he disliked about her? Should she be impressed because
he found her disagreeable enough to be interesting? She
thought of how, a few months ago, the very thought
that Shane Holt could tell her she was a person worth
knowing would have been beyond her wildest dreams—
and how it might still have been, had it been said in
different circumstances. A few months ago, the
possibility of having a hamburger with Shane Holt
would have sent her into a daze of rapture, and she
reflected dryly that, like all the other dreams in her life,
this one, too, was tainted. And all she felt as she
covered up her leftovers and stuffed the wrappings into
the paper bag was a sort of vague depression.

It was a little before eight when they arrived home,
and Lauren was already sleepy. She remembered what
Shane had said about using sleep as an escape, and it
disturbed her, for she did not want to admit—even as a

remote possibility—that he could be right. What she really wanted to do was to go upstairs, have a hot bath, and creep into the comfort of her bed, but she did not dare admit that to him ... and even to herself she suspected that the real reason she wanted to go to bed early was to avoid meeting the celebrities Van was bringing home.

So she helped him bring in the packages, pretending an energy she did not feel, and even tried to help put the purchases away. But Shane knew the house, and the way Marie kept things, so much better than she did that she soon discovered she was doing nothing but getting in the way. After a while she wandered into the living room and settled down on the sofa, pulling up a hassock for her weary legs.

When Shane came into the living room a few moments later the first thing he did was turn on the stereo. His selection was Handel, and Lauren was cautiously thrilled. That was *one* thing she had guessed right about him. His own compositions reflected a definite classical influence, and she had always imagined that his personal tastes would run towards something a little more enduring than hard rock—and that did give them at least one thing in common.

'Handel was my father's favourite,' she commented as he handed her a glass of wine.

'Van said your father was a cellist.'

She nodded. 'I cut my teeth on Bach, Mozart, Haydn ... I was the only kid in kindergarten who could pronounce Shostakovich.' She dropped her eyes to the rich red depth of her glass, remembering. 'Our house was filled with music as far back as I can remember. Verdi, Bizet, Debussy, Grieg ... My mother didn't have a favourite; she loved them all.' She smiled reminiscently, swirling the liquid absently in her glass. 'Wagner, Stravinsky, Beethoven ... always music.' Lilting music, haunting music, music that dreams were made of ... from the cradle her mind had moved in harmony with it; it was only natural that her body should soon follow.

Shane said gently, 'You must miss them very much.'

She looked up, her smile was absent and sad but not bitter. 'Sometimes more than others,' she admitted. 'It wasn't so bad at first, because it seemed a part of them lived on in me every time I danced . . .' How easily she was telling him all this, how naturally her deepest feelings found expression when moved by the one common bond they shared, music. And what a relief it was to look into his eyes and find understanding there, and gentle encouragement. 'Now . . .' But here she faltered, for it occurred to her for the first time that a discussion of her own loss might bring back painful memories for him, and that every other time she had brought up the subject of music it had resulted in a fight. She did not want to end the evening that way.

But he only prompted, watching her steadily, 'Now?'

She lifted her shoulders slightly, again dropping her eyes to her glass. 'I don't know. I seem to think about them more lately, and there's an emptiness there. I know it's not rational, but sometimes I feel as though I let them down, somehow.' And again she shrugged, embarrassed by a confession which sounded childish even to her ears, and uncomfortable that she had somehow been led into confiding in him something which was so personal she had never before ever examined it herself.

She could feel his eyes on her, but she did not meet them. And then he said thoughtfully, 'Sometimes grief is a chain reaction. One loss reminds us of another, and another, and pretty soon we can't see what we have for crying over all we're missing.'

And then Lauren looked at him. 'Is that what happened to you?' she asked softly.

She could not believe she had been so cruel—or so stupid.

A veil fell over his eyes, and the muscle in his jaw tightened. She was prepared for it then—the coldness, the withdrawal, the anger. But he only said, taking a sip of his wine, 'It's chilly in here. How about a fire?'

Without waiting for her answer, he set his glass on the mantle and knelt to light the fire which Van had laid that morning. Lauren, chagrined and desperately needing to atone for her thoughtlessness, tried to move the subject gently back to neutral ground. 'Who's your favourite composer?' she asked.

To her great relief, he took her question in the spirit it was meant, and answered easily. 'I like piano compositions. Chopin and Liszt are my favourites, I guess.'

She smiled secretly to herself, because she would have guessed as much. Somehow knowing that she had been right about him in some ways completely erased the disappointment of the discovery she had made about how wrong she had been about him in others.

And then he surprised her by asking, 'Who's yours? No, let me guess.' He stood and took his wine from the mantle, coming over to her at a relaxed pace. 'Gershwin,' he decided, sitting beside her on the sofa.

She shook her head, smiling. The real answer was, of course, Shane Holt, but on this occasion she decided, wisely, to settle for second best. 'Johann Strauss,' she told him.

The woodsmoke was crisp and fragrant, and the crackling logs provided a harmonious counterpoint to the sleepy background music. The smile in Shane's eyes was relaxed and pleasant as he said, 'All right, everyone's entitled to one mistake. Let me try for two out of three.' He leaned across her to turn down the lamp, and when he straightened up his arm rested casually about her shoulders. The orange and yellow flames danced dreamily on his face and everything else receded into the dim background as he looked at her thoughtfully. 'You like pink champagne,' he decided in a moment, 'designer gowns from New York houses, red roses in a cut glass vase, mountain sunsets, going barefoot, satin sheets . . .'

Lauren interrupted him with a startled laugh. 'Whoa, that's more than three!'

He grinned. 'How am I doing?'

'Terrible,' she told him, her eyes sparkling with the sudden flush of the wine and the firelight and the simple pleasure of being relaxed with him for once. 'Besides, you cheated. Everyone likes designer gowns, but who can afford them? Same with mountain sunsets—what's not to like? But I hate pink champagne.'

His finger gently caressed the edge of her jaw, and his eyes were rich with a warm, relaxed smile. 'But I was right about the roses and going barefoot. What do you think of satin sheets?'

She swallowed hard, very much aware of the light touch of his finger on her face and the warm prickling sensation which was beginning on her neck and travelling down her spine. But she returned lightly, placing her glass on the table, 'I think you just put that in to be cute.'

'I'm never cute.' His finger was absently tracing the curve of her earlobe now, and the touch caused her breath to quicken foolishly; she felt warm all over. Nervously, she brushed at her hair just above his fingers, and he took the hint. His hand left her ear to rest casually upon the back of the sofa again, and she cautiously relaxed.

'Is something wrong with your wine?' he enquired.

'It makes me sleepy,' she told him, and moved a few inches away from him on the pretext of arranging her legs more comfortably on the hassock.

But that strategy had the exact opposite effect from what she had intended. He glanced at her jeaned legs, stretched out straight before her, and commented, 'That's very bad for you, you know.' He set his glass on the table beside hers and slipped his hand beneath her knee, bending it upwards until her foot rested on the hassock. 'Didn't your doctor show you the exercise?'

She nodded, wishing he would remove his hand. It was too easy to imagine that gesture as lover-like, and everything he had done today seemed to have been designed purely to confuse her.

'Then why don't you do them?'

Still his hand was cupped lightly about her knee, and she could feel his eyes upon her, but she kept her own eyes on her hand. Those fingers, strong and gentle, had created the music which had moved her soul, that was the voice she had loved for so many years without knowing and this was the touch which had haunted her secret daydreams. You're star-struck, she told herself derisively, and deliberately stretched her leg out flat again. Grow up.

She responded, a bit more sharply than she should have, 'I don't want to.'

'That's a self-destructive attitude.' And, to her surprise, instead of dropping his hand, he moved it lightly up her thigh and across her abdomen until his fingers circled her waist and rested there. Where his hand had brushed muscles tensed and circulation throbbed, and she felt a quickening of her breath, an alertness and a wariness, and she wanted to look at him but she did not dare.

He solved that problem for her by taking her chin gently between thumb and forefinger and tilting her face upwards to look at him. Her eyes were wide and bright in the firelight as they scanned his, and the rosy colour in her cheeks was more than a reflection of the flames. In his eyes she found only a gentle smile, and the light brush of his finger across her lips made his intention perfectly clear. Yet she was in a quandary. This was Shane Holt, who could have any woman he wanted. This was the man who, only a few days ago, had called her an interfering brat and expressed the wish never to see her again. What was he doing, and why? Shane Holt, vital, attractive, talented, with the world at his feet, could have no interest in an immature, unattractive ex-dancer and present nothing, and she turned her face away quickly, dropping her eyes, just as he started to move closer.

He took this second rebuff in his stride, just as he had the first. He straightened up casually, reached for his glass of wine, and took one or two leisurely sips. Automatically, Lauren did the same. She no longer felt sleepy; in fact, she doubted whether she would sleep at all tonight. Every nerve fibre of her body had suddenly come alive, and she seemed to be more aware of everything around her than she had ever been before in her life. The music seemed clearer, the fragrance of the fire more resonant, the colours—violet and orange and yellow—it generated more translucent and surrealistic, and its crackling and popping sound more melodious. The wine tasted sharp and sweet, and it somehow mixed with the fragrance of his cologne and the slight salty taste the brief touch of his finger had left on her lips to form a subtle aphrodisiac, one whose effect she fought off determinedly. Although his posture beside her was relaxed, still he sat much too close, and the very air around her seemed to throb with electricity.

Then he said mildly, 'Perhaps you would be good enough to tell me just one thing. How do I keep getting my signals crossed?'

Lauren gulped, rather than sipped, her wine, and then took a short, rather unsteady breath to clear her voice. Some part of her told her she was being foolish, this was the chance of a lifetime to live out a fantasy and forget for a moment the harsh reality and that, above all things was what she wanted. But another part warned her that she would be even more foolish to put her faith in dreams again, and so she said trying to sound natural, 'I don't know what you mean.'

'The least you could do,' he returned calmly, 'is not lie to me. You know perfectly well what I mean. I know you're attracted to me—unless everything I ever learned about body language has been a lie, you've been telling me that since the first night we met.' Her colour rose, for of course that was true, and she quickly took another swallow of wine to hide it. He went on, watching her carefully, but with no change whatsoever in the easy inflection of his voice, 'Aside from the fact that I'm mean, arrogant, rude and overbearing—why do you cringe every time I touch you?'

Obviously, she was not going to be able to avoid this very unpleasant conversation. She wished she had the courage to just get up and leave him here—but, truthfully, she did not want to do that either. She forced a little laugh and glanced at him. 'That has nothing to do with it.'

'Good,' Shane said soberly. 'Because I've been trying very hard the past few days to put our rather rough start behind us, and to perhaps give you a little time to discover I'm not really as twisted and ugly as you thought at first.'

Her eyes flew to him and her heart wrenched to see nothing but sincerity on his face. She despised herself for ever having uttered such heartless words, for only now was she beginning to suspect how she might have hurt him. She would have given anything to have taken them back, but apologies never erased harm already done. And all she could do was say quickly, 'No, that's not . . .' And then she dropped her eyes, suppressing a sigh of embarrassment and misery. 'It has nothing to do with you, okay? It's me.'

He enquired simply, 'Do you have some sort of hang-up about men?'

'No!' she answered immediately, but again she could not maintain the eye contact for more than a minute. Miserably, she stared into her wine, the lovely glow of the evening fading fast. She mumbled, inching a little away from him to give veracity to her words, 'I just don't like to be touched, okay? Especially not by Shane Holt, perfect and unattainable, who could remind her by only his presence that she was worthless, unfeminine and undesirable, that she had nothing to offer a man such as he and was unworthy of his notice.

He said firmly, 'No, it's not okay.' He turned to place his empty glass on the table and then back to her again. His tone was matter-of-fact and she was too miserable to look at his eyes. 'Actually, it presents quite a problem. You see, I'm a very demonstrative person.

And as long as you're within three feet of me, you're going to get touched.' To prove it, he slipped his arm about her shoulders again and refused to take the hint when she tried to inch gently away.

She retorted lightly, 'Then I guess the thing to do is to make sure to keep more than three feet between us.'

His fingers tightened slightly on her shoulder. He said quietly, 'For Pete's sake, Lauren, look at me'.

She did, startled and confused, and his expression was serious, as was his tone as he asked gently, 'Why are you doing this to yourself? What are you so afraid of?'

'I'm not afraid of anything,' she answered, and of course he knew it was a lie. She sighed, trying to reach for something closer to the truth which would satisfy him without making her more vulnerable than she already felt. 'Look, it's just that I have a lot on my mind right now, a lot of adjusting to do . . .'

'Let me help,' he suggested softly.

She caught her breath, examining his face for some sign of lightness or teasing, startled to find neither. She blurted, without thinking, 'Why should you care?'

His sigh was of barely restrained impatience. 'Because I'm not really so awful and I just do, all right? You have got one rock-bottom self-image, lady, heaven knows why, and it's something we're going to start to work on right now.' There was a firm decision in his tone as he took both her shoulders and turned her to face him. 'So,' he suggested mildly, 'you'd better get used to the possibility of being touched.'

Some of that awful seriousness had gone out of his voice, and she thought she could deal with him more easily on this level. She said lightly, 'I don't deny my self-image could use a little improvement, but I don't think there's anything *you* can do about it. So if you don't mind . . .' Lauren looked meaningfully at his hands, which still gripped her shoulders.

'On the contrary,' he replied softly, and there was a strange, provocative look in his eye. 'There's a great deal I can do about it.' Then he released her shoulders and extended his hand palm upwards to her. 'Give me your hand,' he demanded. 'We'll start with a little touch therapy.'

She hesitated, alarm striking her with a very definite uncertainty about his intentions, and when she glanced at him there was a twinkle of amusement in his eye. 'Come on,' he urged, closing his fingers about her hand. 'I promise I won't do anything obscene . . . not for a while yet, anyway.'

Lauren laughed nervously. 'That's supposed to be reassuring?'

'No,' he replied, 'that's supposed to be stimulating.'

Her laugh was more natural that time, and Shane brushed his hand lightly across her hair, smiling. She thought he was teasing, and that he would surely let the joke drop, and she was surprised when he increased the light pressure of his fingers on her hand and guided it gently to his face. 'The first step,' he told her, 'in learning to accept pleasure is learning to give it.'

'Where did you learn that?' she retorted lightly, trying to draw her hand away. 'E.S.T.? Nude encounter groups?'

His eyes were perfectly bland. 'Would you prefer nude encounter? It's just as effective.'

'And just as ridiculous,' she replied, making a real effort now to free her hand, only to have his fingers tighten about it in response. Her cheeks were hot and her heart was tripping rapidly in her chest.

'Relax,' he commanded, and deliberately uncurled her fingers one by one, placing her hand flat against his face. 'This is serious.'

'This is silly,' she answered uncomfortably. She was uncertain whether the tightening within her stomach was due to nervousness or the determined tone of his voice, or the sensuous intent in his eyes—or perhaps all. A moment of indecision convinced her that it would be much more embarrassing to try to break away than to go along with his little game, and she tried to force herself to relax and take it lightly, letting her hand rest without resistance on the rough plane of his face. 'Now what?' she demanded.

'Close your eyes,' he ordered, and she found that a suggestion which was easy to comply with. She could not bear to look at him throughout this ridiculous charade, with her face scarlet and her eyes miserable with embarrassment, knowing that his fingers on her wrist measured every increment of her pulse. She thought it might be easier, after all, to make a scene and break away.

'I don't like this,' she warned, and then he moved her hand, urging her fingers to lightly explore the breadth of his forehead, the soft fall of hair there, the smooth arch of his eyebrows and then, very delicately, across his closed lids ... her fingers were unsteady, and she was not certain whether that was due to nervousness or to the other emotion which was tightening steadily within her and was too fragile to be defined. She felt the need to break the mood, and she said, 'I feel stupid.'

'I like it.' Gently, Shane urged her fingers downward, slowly over his cheeks; she felt the rough texture of his skin where his face darkened into five o'clock shadow, and the surprising softness of the bridge of his nose and the uneven little bump there, and then she was aware that her fingers were moving and exploring on their own, without his encouragement, and that the tactile pleasure of so simple an exercise was tingling like electricity in the tips of her fingers and tripling the beat of her pulse. She deliberately stopped, and opened her eyes.

'Do you do this with every woman you meet?' she asked. She had intended to break the mood and shatter the vibrant, totally unexpected atmosphere of sensuality which had surrounded them, but her voice was too soft and breathless to communicate anything other than encouragement.

Shane replied silkily, lightly striking the back of her hand with his forefinger, 'I wish someone would introduce me to all these women you seem to think I know. It probably would have saved me a lot of lonely nights.'

And then, deliberately, he guided her trembling fingers across his face, over the cleft of his chin, around the softness of his parted lips. Lauren caught her breath involuntarily and her eyes closed as he drew one finger inside his mouth.

New vistas of sensuality opened up to her in the warm moisture of his mouth, the gentle sucking motion encompassed the tip of another finger, and then another ... The light pressure of smooth, even teeth, the warm caress of his tongue exploring nail beds and tingling the tips of her fingers. Her breath was suddenly shallow and uneven, a light film of perspiration broke out across her throat and spread to her chest; the room was over-warm. No parts of their bodies touched except their fingers and his lips, but behind her closed eyes incredible images were forming.

She drew her fingers away and opened her eyes, trying once again to break the mood. But it was too late. Already her fingers, still moist from the recesses of his mouth, were trailing downwards across his throat, exploring the rough texture of his skin and the uneven ridges of his throat, the silky tuft of hair that appeared at the hollow where the collarbone separated, and his eyes were smoky and slightly hooded, offering no discouragement. 'How,' she managed breathlessly, almost in a whisper, 'how is this supposed to help my self-image?'

'Very simply.' His voice was husky and his hand left hers to travel lightly up the course of her arm, his fingers playing with feather-touches across her face and threading her hair. 'You must know you're very valuable to me, because I've never gone to so much trouble for a kiss before.'

More than anything at that moment she wanted him to kiss her. Her body cried out for it, and more, as both her hands travelled shyly up his arms to caress the broad expanse of his shoulders. But if Shane sensed her impatience he chose to ignore it, and he simply whispered, 'Close your eyes.'

Lauren felt no urge to disobey, and then his fingers were upon her body as hers had been upon his, brushing, exploring, lightly caressing . . . she shivered and gave herself over to the experience.

His hands were upon her face now, and she was amazed at the softness of them, the delicacy with which he stroked her brow and her eyelids, traced the curvature of her nose and the square outline of her jaw. The tension flowed from her arms and she let her hands wander down to his chest, to the brief expanse of bare skin there and then to firm muscles, across his breast where her palm discovered the sturdy throb of his heart. His sweater was like silk beneath her fingers, but it was so thin she could feel the heat of his body through it and the soft mat of hair . . . no, it was richer than silk, it was like the soft fur of a warm animal, and she let her fingers travel luxuriously across the full breadth of it, the strength of his ribcage, the firmness of his abdomen, resting when the softness melted into the new texture of a leather belt, and then his hands left her face to begin a new exploration of his own.

Until tonight Lauren had felt unfeminine and unwanted, and it was true her self-image had suffered badly. But under the sensual touch of Shane's fingers she discovered there was nothing whatsoever wrong with her libido, for she was helpless against the response he generated within her. His touch was so light it was more of a promise than a fact as it travelled slowly across her ribs, across her thighs, upwards to her breasts. And there, with a gentle circular motion, his fingers discovered the tautness of her nipples and caressed, sending electric waves of tingling sensation through her. Every fibre of her body was alert and painfully aware of him, yet she was motionless, weak, and anything other than the physical response which overwhelmed her was beyond her capabilities.

He took her face between both hands, very gently, and she could not even open her eyes. She felt his nearness by the warmth of his breath upon her parted lips; her heart began to thud in her throat and she could no longer breathe, and then, lightly, so lightly it was almost a whisper, she felt his tongue flicker along her lower lip.

A muffled sound escaped her, whether of expectation or surprise she did not know. Heat flamed through her and yearning tightened in her chest and spread slowly to her stomach as she felt his tongue brush delicately across her teeth and the moist portion of her inner lip. Her hands tightened upon his waist, and just as she expected his lips to clasp fully upon hers, he said softly, 'Unless we want to finish this with an audience, I think we'd better stop now.'

Shock reverberated through her as his hands left her face and closed about her hands, which were still on his waist. She opened her eyes, but nothing was clear, everything still pounded in a foggy haze of passion and expectancy and yearning so cruelly unfulfilled. She could not believe that he was removing her hands from his waist, that even now he was standing and pulling her to her feet. And then she heard voices outside and a key in the lock and she thought she understood.

His smile was regretful and in his eyes she saw the same sort of confusion and impatience which was in her own. 'Try to remember,' he advised gently as he released her hands, 'that you're leaving me in the same condition.'

And then he turned to greet Van.

CHAPTER FIVE

LAUREN turned away quickly, knowing that one glimpse of her flushed face and rumpled hair would give her hosts a perfect picture of what had been going on on the sofa before their arrival. Nervously, she smoothed her hair and took a couple of deep breaths while Shane distracted their attention with light greetings and trivial questions about the drive and the traffic at the airport. The other voices joined those of Marie and Van in the foyer, and Lauren turned to see Angel Roberts.

Angel was one of those incredibly beautiful women who seem to be the exclusive products of Nashville or Los Angeles recording studios. Her silver-blonde hair fell smooth and straight to her hips, only the minimun of make-up adorned her small, lovely face, and a pair of smoky-lensed sunglasses rested atop her head. She stepped immediately into Shane's arms, and Lauren watched incredulously as he bent and kissed her tenderly on the lips, murmuring, 'You're as gorgeous as ever.'

Angel smiled up at him, caressing his neck affectionately, and answered, 'You're looking pretty fit yourself. Wow, it's been a long time!'

'Two years,' answered Shane, and Lauren was stunned into childish incredulity as she watched them, thinking ridiculously, She got the kiss that was meant for me. Shane is holding her and touching her just as he did me a moment ago ... and what she felt was indignation mixed with a very definite jealousy.

And then she was ashamed of herself. She had been in show business long enough to know that such demonstrations of affection were not only common, they were almost mandatory—and ultimately meaningless. She herself had played out many such scenes.

Once, new to life backstage, she had expressed astonishment at all the hugging and kissing that went on among perfect strangers at a theatre party, and a veteran had told her with a careless grin, 'With the kind of life we lead, you have to take it when you can get it'—then he proceeded to proposition her most charmingly. Of course she was being irrational over Shane's reaction to Angel, and she told herself she would not have even noticed it if she hadn't been in such a state of heightened sexual awareness—and if Angel had not been quite so beautiful.

And then, as Shane was slipping off Angel's raccoon jacket, Van said, 'Angel, I want you to meet a dear friend of mine.' He extended his hand and drew Lauren forward. 'Angel Roberts, Lauren Davis.' Two other members of her band were with her, a tall, studious man with frizzy red hair, called Chris, and an older, positively huge gentleman with a bristly beard and a ringing laugh by the name of Chuck. Lauren was introduced all around, but she did not really pay much attention because, after greeting Lauren pleasantly, Angel had turned to Shane and was engaging him in soft, intimate conversation as he led her across the room with an arm about her waist.

Afterwards there was the usual confusion of drinks being poured and everyone talking at once as six people tried to catch up on all the news and witty gossip, exclusive to their industry, and Lauren quite naturally felt excluded. Angel monopolised Shane's attention—as well as that of everyone else in the room—with no effort at all, but Lauren could not really resent her for it. She was simply that type of woman, and she could not have reached such a degree of success if she had been different. But, Lauren thought bleakly, if she was expected to compete with Angel Roberts there simply was no contest. And Shane seemed to have forgotten that Lauren existed.

Chuck lowered his large frame on to the sofa beside her and dropped a companionable hand on her knee.

'So, sweetie,' he invited, 'what do you do? Sing? Play? Or . . .' his grin was not in the least insulting, 'do you just hang around to keep old Shane happy?'

Lauren could not really be offended by the insinuating remark or by the hand on her knee; it was show talk from a show person, she was used to it. That was not what bothered her. It was the necessity of explaining to a stranger that she was no part of this scene, that she did not really belong here amidst all the success and bright lights, that she was, in fact, nothing. 'I'm—I was,' she corrected painfully, 'a dancer. Touring shows, off Broadway. They call us gypsies.'

'Hey, is that right? That's cute.' He sipped from his drink, his bright eyes expressing lively interest in everyone and everything about him. Lauren just happened to be in the path of an enquiring mind. 'What do you mean, "you were"? Did you retire or something? Get too old for the circuit?'

Van had made something of the same observation while she was still in hospital, trying to comfort her by pointing out that, at twenty-six, her career as a dancer was almost over anyway. It had been no comfort. Van did not understand, any more than this well-intentioned stranger could, that the love of performing was not circumscribed by age and that she would have danced for ever if she could have.

'No,' she said rather shortly. 'I had an accident—a knee injury, and surgery. I can't dance any more.'

It never failed to amaze her to hear her own voice uttering those fatal words, those earth-shattering words, and every time it was like the first time. But Chuck only looked mildly amused, and said, 'Hey, no kidding? I did that once. Pulled a muscle or something, right in the middle of a number in front of a packed-out house. Tried to jump over an amplifier and fell off the damn stage. Hey, Chris,' he turned to slap Chris on the arm, laughing, 'you remember that, man? Remember how old Archie was running around screaming I was dead when the cable came loose and sparks were flying all over the place?' He turned back to Lauren, his eyes dancing madly with the memory and the laughter he had elicited from everyone else. 'Same thing.'

Lauren tried to smile, but she thought bleakly, No, it's not. It's not the same at all. Because when you picked yourself up you could get right back on stage and your life wasn't over, your world wasn't changed . . .

The laughter and the recapping of memories went on about her and she tried to look polite and interested. In fact she felt only isolated, and vaguely depressed. What did any of these people know about heartbreak? She was glad when the party began to make its way to the music room and she was able to slip away unnoticed to her room.

It was not until she was there that she discovered one other reason for her mounting depression. She suddenly remembered that Angel had done a duet with Shane on his last album entitled *Just Another Memory*. She wondered how deep the relationship went. But it was none of her business, and certainly none of her concern. After all, Shane had managed his life quite well before Lauren Davis had come into it—as he had so bitingly pointed out not very long ago.

The beat of drums and the throb of bass pounded in the walls, and Lauren turned over on her side, trying to get comfortable even if she couldn't sleep. She thought of them all down there, making music and having a good time, and she wondered if Shane were playing one of the instruments. She wondered if he would sing, and if he would be laughing with Angel and exchanging intimate glances.

She gave a little groan of impatience with herself and turned over on her back, momentarily drawing the pillow over her head to block out the sounds from below. But then she pushed the pillow away and turned her face thoughtfully towards the door, wondering about Shane, trying to figure him out. What had it all meant, today, and this evening . . . why the sudden change in attitude towards her, why the professed interest in her well-being, and above all, why, if he could have a woman like Angel Roberts, would he bother with Lauren? Was he really that lonely, or that bored? He had appeared to be neither in the short time she had observed him. Then perhaps he was simply one of those men who didn't like to be rebuffed and had made up his mind that first time she had turned away from him to have her just for the sake of his ego. She hoped that was not the case, because she hated to play those stupid games and she certainly had no intention of serving as balm to Shane Holt's ego. No, more likely it was something much simpler . . . what had he said today? 'Go with the impulse and sort out your mistakes later.' Yes, that was the way Shane would think, and Lauren's only mistake had been in taking him too seriously.

She tried to put him out of her mind, but she lay awake for a long, long time, listening to the music.

'Lauren.' In her dreams she imagined Shane's voice, soft and silky, in her ear. In her dream she felt his fingers lightly brush her hair away from her cheek, and heard him whisper her name again. She felt the warmth of his breath on her face, and his hands cupping her shoulders and lifting, drawing her close to him . . .

Only this was no dream. She opened her eyes sleepily, and Shane's three fingers across her lips muffled her startled gasp. 'Ssh,' he said softly, 'everyone else is still asleep.'

Her eyes opened wide, straining to make out his face in the foggy dark, and she sat up straight, pulling the blanket up high under her chin. 'What,' she whispered hoarsely as he cautiously removed his fingers, 'what are you doing here?'

'Time to get up,' he returned cheerfully. 'We have a date to go walking, remember?'

She stared at him. 'You're crazy! It's the middle of the night!'

'Lower your voice.' He stood and drew the curtains, letting in only a sparse amount of hazy light. 'It's after seven,' he told her. 'The best part of the morning is already gone.'

Lauren groaned and sank back into the pillows, drawing the blanket securely around her shoulders. 'You *are* crazy,' she mumbled. 'Go away!'

'Hurry and get dressed,' he said, starting for the door. 'I'll wait for you downstairs.'

'Don't hold your breath!'

Suddenly the covers were jerked off the bed, exposing her scantily clad body to the chill morning air, and as she sat up in shock and indignation he began to tickle her bare feet ruthlessly. Immediately his hand clapped over her mouth to muffle her squeals, and he sat beside her, one arm about her to still her struggles, his eyes dancing with laughter. 'There's a house full of people,' he warned, 'who are only going to think the worst if they come bursting in here to rescue you and find us together. Don't you care about your reputation?'

She shook her head defiantly against the clasp of his hand, her eyes glowering.

'Well, I care about mine,' he told her, cautiously removing his hand. 'So show a little consideration.'

'Me?' She lowered her voice as his hand moved warningly near her mouth again. '*You're* the one who came bursting in here without knocking—again—and woke me up—*again*, and took my blankets and left me freezing!'

Though she shivered in her thin satin pyjamas, she was far from cold inside. Her colour was high and she felt alert and ready for anything, and Shane's wool-clad arm about her waist was scratchy and warm. Then a slow grin crept across his features in the dark, and he slipped his other arm about her, drawing her firmly into the circle of his chest. 'You don't feel a bit cold to me,' he said. 'As a matter of fact, you're the second warmest thing I've held in my arms today.'

The wool jacket smelled of woodsmoke and

masculinity, and the feel of his arms about her, the nearness of him, caused her heart to pound faster. But she placed her hand against his chest as though to push away and looked up at him suspiciously. 'Second warmest?'

'Well,' he confessed, 'there was this old grey tomcat that wandered into the backyard at the crack of dawn. However, he wasn't wearing anything nearly as sexy as you are.'

Lauren clasped both his wrists firmly and moved his hands away, even though a tingling flush was beginning to warm her entire body. 'If this is another one of your attempts to improve my self image,' she told him firmly, 'thanks, but no, thanks.'

Shane's eyes twinkled as he touched her nose lightly. 'The best is yet to come,' he promised, and she felt an automatic and completely uncontrollable clench of anticipation in her chest. He took a firm hold on her hands and stood, pulling her with him. 'If you're not down in five minutes,' he told her, 'I'm coming back up.'

'Bring a jacket,' he added over his shoulder as he reached the door. 'It's cold out.'

Until he had left, Lauren stood stubbornly in the centre of the floor, but as soon as the door closed behind him she hurried to her dresser and pulled out a pair of camel-coloured corduroy slacks and a white cable-knit sweater. She dressed quickly—including hiking boots—and braided her hair into a single loose ponytail at the nape of her neck. Then she grabbed a light flannel jacket and descended the stairs, to meet him in the kitchen fully within his five-minute deadline.

'That's what I like,' he told her with a grin, opening the back door for her, 'punctuality.'

Fog had crept down from the mountains, damp and cold. It brushed across her face like silky cobwebs, clinging to her hair and filling her nostrils with a moist, woodsy scent which was as provocative as it was mysterious. She hesitated on the step, straining her eyes to penetrate the nebulous expanse of grey. 'Are you sure you want to go out in this?' she asked.

Shane chuckled a little and slipped his arms about her waist. 'I'm sure I don't want to go alone.'

It was like stepping into another world, silent and shrouded except for the soft sounds of dew dripping off the bushes and their own muffled, far-away footsteps. The fog sealed itself around them like a veil, moving with them yet encapsulating them in a private space which included nothing but their two bodies, side by side, two solid objects in a formless void, gently muting other sensory input exclusive to themselves. Automatically, Lauren's arm went about his waist—not only because it was awkward to walk otherwise, but because she liked the security of his broad back beneath her arm and the warmth of his closeness.

She felt his fingers tighten upon her ribs in response to her touch, and then he said softly, 'I almost came up to your room last night.'

Her heart gave a little lurch, she caught her breath and tried to make out the expression on his face in the mist. But his next words calmed her pulse and drained away the flush of anticipation as he explained, 'To see why you cut out on us so early. I thought that kind of jam session would be just what you liked.'

She shrugged, feeling foolish and annoyed that she had read a meaning into his words which was not intended. 'I could hear it just as well from upstairs.'

'Kept you awake, did we?'

'For a while,' she answered negligently. Then, 'Was that you on one of the instruments?'

'The keyboards,' he answered without much interest, 'for a while. As a matter of fact, I turned in early myself.'

'Is that right?' The words were out before she knew it. 'Alone?'

He stopped, looking at her with startled amusement, and she wished the fog would cover her right then and let her melt into nothingness. At least it shielded her scarlet face and wretched embarrassment as Shane asked incredulously, 'Was I supposed to do otherwise?'

She dropped her arm from about his waist, but he refused to release her. She could feel his eyes, peering at her in the mist, and then he laughed. 'Good lord,' he exclaimed softly, 'you must mean Angel!' And then he laughed again. 'You *do* mean Angel! You're jealous!'

'I am not!' She broke away from him then, but the only one she was angry with was herself. How could she have been so stupid? She was acting like a thirteen-year-old again, and the worst was, she did not really feel that way at all, it was just that her impulsive speech was always landing her in trouble . . . She smoothed away a damp tendril of hair from her face and looked at him, defiantly pushing the miserable embarrassment behind her and explaining calmly, 'There's nothing to be jealous about. I was just curious, that's all. I didn't mean to infringe on your privacy . . . again.'

His smile was tender, as was the gesture as he reached up to once again smooth away the strand of hair which had strayed over her cheek. 'You don't have to apologise,' he said. 'It's been a long time since anyone was jealous of me, and I rather like it.'

Lauren started walking again, shoving her hands into her pockets to prevent physical contact, and continuing in a calm, matter-of-fact tone, 'It's really none of my business, I know. But you two seemed so friendly, I just assumed . . .'

'Well, you assumed wrong.' He took her hand from her pocket and closed his own firmly about it. There was a new inflection of seriousness to his voice which made an inexplicable little shiver tingle down her spine as he told her, 'Angel and I have shared many things in the past, but I assure you, a bed wasn't one of them.'

Now she was curious. There was something about the sobriety in his voice, the sincerity which indicated to her that her opinion was important to him—the warm clasp of his hand about hers, and perhaps, the secrecy of the fog itself which seemed to invite confidences. For the first time, he had actually brought up the subject of his past without reticence or anger, and that encouraged Lauren, inviting closeness somehow. She had to ask, 'What kind of things?'

But then she sensed a withdrawal in him, as though his mind were flickering over those remembrances and sharply turning away from the pain. The sudden tension was communicated from the muscles of his arm to his hand about hers, and he answered only, 'Life in the fast lane.'

She glanced at him, for that was an enigmatic reply if ever there had been one, but she dared not pursue it. She said instead, trying to find a way to relax the tension she felt from him and bring him back to her, 'So what are the plans for the day?'

For just a moment longer, Shane seemed to be lost in some dark world of his own, but then he looked at her and smiled. 'I don't know. What do you want to do?'

She gave a nervous little laugh, for still some measure of awkwardness clung to her from her *faux pas* of a moment ago, and she was more aware than she would have liked to have been of the danger of pushing him away again. She said, 'No, I meant with you and the band. More jam sessions? Big production meetings? What?'

He said, 'I don't know. They're Van's guests, I don't have anything to do with it.'

She looked at him in surprise. 'Oh, but I thought——'

'That's what you get for thinking again,' he replied firmly. 'Look, let's not talk about Angel any more. I'm sure she's not giving us a second thought, so why should we waste time with her?' Both of his hands rested firmly on her waist as he helped her up a small, rocky incline, and there, beneath a bare, gnarled tree, they stopped.

The fog churned upwards about their feet, obscuring everything except the small patch of rocky grass on which they stood and the knotted white limbs of the tree which seemed to disappear into the clouds about six feet upwards. The wet, cold air was tinted with the smells of moss, decaying leaves, and dark earth, all mingled into the rich broth of the fog, and it was as though they stood upon a precipice at the top of the world . . . and suddenly a line from one of Shane's songs trailed across her mind like the tendrils of the fog: Nothing below you, nothing above/Take what you can where you find it/Nothing behind so you/let yourself love/and don't turn away till you've tried it . . .

She smiled a little, embarrassed for her secret indulgence, and leaned against the tree, her hands flat against its barkless, knotted surface. 'It's like being on another planet,' she said softly.

Shane leaned over her, his hand resting on the tree above her shoulder, smiling softly. Drops of moisture clung to his face and glistened dully in his hair and every fibre of her body was aware of him, misty and nebulous, like a ghost or a dream too long treasured to be real, yet solid and only inches away from her. She knew only seconds separated the warmth of his lips from hers, yet something of the night before crept back to her—something which had meant so much to her yet so little to him, and she was unsure. Again the line from his song haunted her, *Take what you can where you find it*—and as much as she wanted to follow that advice, something restrained her. She said carefully, watching him steadily, 'Are we about to begin lesson two on my programme of self-improvement?'

Some of the warmth faded from his eyes; just as she had intended, the mood was broken. He simply brushed one finger lightly across her cheek, not straightening or otherwise putting any more physical distance between them, and answered, 'Since the first one seems to have had so little effect, I guess not.'

Disappointment tasted bitter in her throat, even though she had invited it. She really did not know what she wanted any more, for since meeting him her entire sense of values had been turned upside down. She only knew she could not bear being mocked by him any longer, or teased, or taken lightly. She pressed her palms flat against the surface of the tree as though to draw courage from its timeless strength, and took a breath, her eyes clear and steady as she looked at him. 'Look,' she said evenly, 'we're both adults here——'

'Or at least one of us is,' he interrupted with a dry smile.

Lauren dropped her eyes briefly. 'All right,' she admitted. 'I know I've been acting like a child lately, and I deserved that.'

'That's all right.' Lightly, his fingers brushed the droplets of fog from her fringe. His voice was soft and melodious against the gentle dripping of the branches and the far-away crash of undergrowth which echoed with the movements of some small bird or animal. 'I suppose I've been caught acting something less than my full thirty-three years the last few days, too. So,' he straightened up decisively, 'you want us to talk like adults, we'll talk like adults. I like your body; what's wrong with that?'

She gave a nervous, startled little laugh. 'Be serious!'

'I am serious.' And his eyes reflected that he was. 'Lauren . . .' He hesitated there, and his brows came together slightly, as though with the difficulty of finding just the right words to express his thought. 'Somehow,' he continued slowly, 'you seem to have gotten the impression that just because you've lost one part of what you were, none of you is any good any more. Maybe it's worse because it was a physical thing— maybe your whole sense of identity was wrapped up in your dancing, and you're letting that reflect now on every aspect of your physical life . . . you see yourself as dull and unattractive and undesirable, and Lauren, I'm trying to tell you that's simply not so.'

She caught her breath softly because, once again, he had touched with a few simple words the very core of a hidden truth within her, just as he had so many times before with his music. She wanted to reach out to him then in tenderness and gratitude, to simply hold him and thank him for the years he had given to her which had culminated in this moment ... but suddenly the mood changed.

His lips tightened dryly in an expression which was half apology, half self-deprecation. 'I know,' he said, 'I'm talking like a college professor again.' And then he touched her nose playfully. 'I've never had to convince a woman with words before that I find her desirable; there's usually a much more direct way.'

Lauren stuffed her hands into her pockets again, made uncomfortable by the frankly sensual gleam in his eye and the sudden change of mood. She said, steeling her nerves against the quiver of anticipation which had started within her, 'I'm not fishing for compliments.'

'You're going to get them anyway,' he returned, very casually. His tone was matter-of-fact, but his eyes touched every part of her, his words catalogued, and each glance was like a caress which brought her senses to tingling life. 'You have a beautiful face, and your eyes are so sad and tender—and then so stormy and defiant—sometimes dreamy, sometimes wild, first like an angel and then like a hellcat ... those eyes could break a man's heart. Your hair, when it's loose and straight and falling about your face, makes me think what it would look like tangled on my pillow and in my face and my eyes and mouth ...' She tensed, even her breathing stilling in her throat with the leap of her pulses and the rush of life through her veins, and each of his words paralysed her with throbbing sensuality more intense than a caress, for his eyes took her to places her hands dared not go. His voice fell a fraction, became more husky, the light in his eyes deeper and filled with unmistakable intent. 'When your nostrils flare, like they're doing now, you remind me of a wild filly begging to be tamed, and that scent you wear—gardenia?—makes me think of things hot and humid and very physical, and the contrast of cool sheets and silver moonlight ...' She could not believe this. This man had the power to arouse her without a single touch, with only a glance, only a phrase ... This man was the master of words and poetry, he had been doing it to her since she had heard his first song and she should not be surprised at the effect now. 'Your neck,' he said softly, 'is one the most beautiful things I've ever seen, a work of art. And your ...'

His eyes moved downward, and she knew she had to stop it now. Heat was flaming in her cheeks and a wild pulse throbbed in her throat and her voice was high and breathless as she exclaimed, 'My! You haven't lost your touch with prose, have you?'

Shane smiled lazily, and his hands came forward to rest lightly on her hips. 'In summary,' he said, exerting a gentle pressure with his hands which caused her to sway towards him slightly, 'I find you have a perfectly delightful little body—despite the absence of twenty or so pounds.'

'Ten,' she corrected hastily, and tried to move away.

'The more there is of you, the better I'll like it.' And she felt the firm pressure of his thumbs against her hipbones and his fingers on the small of her back, and she could not have moved even if she desired to—which she did no longer. In his eyes was a gentle light clear with meaning, and he said softly, 'Are you convinced?' But, without waiting for an answer, Shane bent his head and his lips were upon hers.

A sound formed, low in her throat, but it was mingled with his indrawn breath and lost. It was a sound of release, of wonder, of slowly spiralling pleasure which melted throughout her body until she felt as weak and formless as the fog, wrapped around him, melding into him, becoming a part of him. There was only the softness and the warmth of his lips upon hers, the heat which fanned her body, the tremulous, paralysing sensations which pulsed in pinpoints of light behind her closed eyes, and abrupt stilling of everything within her—her breath, her heartbeat, her will and her reason—it was more than she had ever imagined, and it was all. Even her arms were limp at her sides, and her lips moulding helplessly to the demand of his, receiving him, letting the sensations move her into glowing, tingling, pulsing awareness of him and of herself at the point where she became a part of him and was lost.

When he drew away, slowly, reluctantly, and almost cautiously, she became aware that at no time had any parts of their bodies touched except their lips, and Shane's hands, steady and strong, upon her hips. She felt stunned and weak; she knew that if he moved, or for one moment relaxed the supporting pressure of his hands, she would collapse against his chest and lie there, still and helpless, until his touch brought her to life again. But his hands remained steady, the gentle, tender light in his eyes held her hypnotised just as his kiss had done, just as his words had done before that. He said softly, 'That was definitely worth waiting for.'

It had never happened to her like this before. Not ever. Still she was trembling inside, still she glowed with an impatient flush which denied the cold and the damp which surrounded her, still the taste of him was on her lips and her mouth pulsed with the warmth of his. Yet all the events which had lead up to this moment came crowding in on her, and with them, confusion. This was Shane Holt, the man of magical words and legendary music, strong, attractive, vital ... he could have any woman he wanted. This was the man who had despised her from the moment they met, who had made her the victim of his cruel tongue on more than one occasion, and who had, overnight, done an about-face ... why? None of it made sense.

Some of the passion ebbed away with the slow return of reason, and strength and caution took its place. Her hands closed over his and removed their hold; she turned away. The fingers which closed about her waist were swift and sure, but his voice was hesitant as he queried, 'Lauren?'

Her body was turned away from him, her arm stretched behind her by the hold he had on her wrist.

The fog was beginning to break up, and in the distance silver beams of sunlight fell in straight, iridescent lines through the dense foilage, refracted by the mist and dancing like prismed diamonds on waxy leaves, a fairy-tale setting, like the stage set for the Enchanted Forest scene in *Camelot* . . . or like the promise of hope for dreams come true. But when she turned her head to look at him there was only caution in her eyes, simple curiosity. She asked carefully, 'Why are you doing this?'

In his face was nothing but confusion. 'What do you mean? I told you——'

Lauren shook her head, withdrawing her hand and cupping both her elbows to stop a shiver which was the result of draining passion and sudden nervousness. Her voice was more curt than she had intended as she interrupted, 'I know what you said. Pretty words. I want to know the real reason. What kind of game are you playing?'

In his eyes she was surprised to find disappointment, and something that suspiciously resembled hurt. He let his hand drop back to his side, 'No game,' he answered simply, honestly. 'I just thought . . . hell, I don't know what I thought.' His voice sounded tired. 'That we could be friends, maybe. That we could know each other better, at least.'

Oh, there were dozens of witty retorts she could have made, such as the physical limitations of simple 'friendship' and how far he was willing to go to 'know her better', but she sensed strongly that this was not the time for them, and she felt no urge to be flippant. She simply looked at him, searching his face anxiously, and she insisted, 'But *why*? Why the sudden change? It doesn't make sense, you know it doesn't. Can you blame me for wondering?'

His features relaxed into a vague, rather sad half-smile. 'No,' he admitted, 'I don't suppose I can blame you, but does everything have to make sense?' And then he hesitated, for her eyes told him that answer was not good enough. In his eyes in the next few moments she saw thoughtfulness, frustration, helplessness, and, finally, a rueful smile as he said, 'Maybe that's one reason. Because you're always asking me questions I can't answer.'

He took a few steps away from her, and Lauren thought the subject was closed, that now they would walk silently back to the house with everything unsettled between them and she would be left in a state of turmoil. Shane reached up and absently broke a twig off a branch of the tree; he held it in his hand a moment before tossing it away. And then he said, without looking at her, 'I know when we first met I acted like—well, like everything you called me. And it's true I didn't like you; you made me furious and there were all kinds of good reasons why I acted the way I did—and none of them really matter now. You see . . .' He turned, and the expression on his face was cautious, as though he were entrusting her with a confidence yet was afraid of revealing too much. 'For the past few years I've led a very—protected life. I know it sounds stupid, but that's the way I chose to arrange things. I have a few good friends who stay my friends by playing by my rules and running interference for me when strangers start getting too personal—or too curious. So when you came bursting on the scene with your impertinent questions and outrageous demands, you caught me completely off guard. I overreacted.' He dropped his eyes briefly. 'I—do that sometimes, no excuses.' He released a short breath. 'I don't know.'

She thought he would leave it with that very ineloquent finish, and without ever having really answered her question. But then he looked at her again and went on, 'What happened?' A small, dry smile tightened one corner of his lips. 'You got to me, I guess, eventually. Believe it or not, I don't really enjoy acting like an ass, and some of the things you said . . . well, they hurt,' he admitted bluntly. 'And then I took another look at you and, Lauren, I saw so much of myself there . . . it made a difference. Can you understand any of what I'm saying?'

She nodded, slowly, but in truth, though some of her questions had been answered, just as many new ones had opened up. What did he mean about seeing himself in her? What could they possibly have in common besides the fact that she loved his music and he resented any mention of it? And why did he feel it necessary to protect himself from strangers and ex-fans . . . was there really any reason good enough to justify the way he had acted the day he had discovered her playing his record? But she could see what this simple confession and apology had cost him, and she was not about to press for details. She would accept it because that was all he was offering, and be glad that he had given her that much.

'Look,' he said with another brief, frustrated sigh, 'I'm not promising I'll behave any better in the future, or—well, I'm not promising anything. But I don't want you to think I've been using you, or that I've been anything less than honest about my reasons for wanting to make peace. Fair enough?'

Lauren managed a smile that was almost natural as she came towards him, hands in pockets, and agreed, 'Fair enough.'

His eyes crinkled in a smile of welcome and relief as he slipped his arm about her waist and they started down the hill. After all, what more could she ask? It was a dream come true, just the chance to know him . . . and she did want to know him, all of him. There were yet so many questions unanswered, so many things about him she needed to understand, and the need to know was stronger than ever.

And then, midway down the hill, Shane commented casually, 'Notice anything different?'

She looked at him in confusion. 'About what?'

He replied negligently, without looking at her, 'You're forgetting to limp.'

She stopped, looked at him, and then, incredulously,

at her own legs. Then she burst into astonished laughter, for, of course, he was perfectly right.

His eyes twinkled as he looked down at her. 'What do you think about my programme of self-improvement now?'

She laughed again, now in pure delight, and impulsively threw her arms about his neck. He responded with a happy laugh of his own and an embrace which was sure and strong—but much too brief. Then they made their way back to the house at a bright, easy pace.

CHAPTER SIX

BREAKFAST was the beginning of a chaotic day—and, in fact, it was only a preview of a hectic week. Confusion was inevitable with seven people under one roof, but when five of those people were musicians and three of them performing artists utter pandemonium was the result. For the first time, Marie actually needed her help with the housework and the meals, and Lauren enjoyed feeling useful. She also enjoyed the high-spirited atmosphere that pervaded the house, the juvenile antics of their house guests which were common among people who worked hard and relaxed frantically—the incredible stories, the unexpected lapses into song and improvisation, the music that pounded through the house far into the night.

She and Shane were rarely alone again during that week, and even when they were there was no hint of a repetition of their last encounter together. When Lauren was not busy with Marie preparing three meals a day for seven or shopping or dusting or vacuuming, Shane was busy in the music room or involved in a conversation with one or more of their guests. Their morning walks remained a routine, but very often they were accompanied by Angel or the two men, and even when they were alone Shane seemed preoccupied and ill at ease. Lauren suspected that for some reason the visit of these old friends of his had made him nervous.

It was true that the band members did not always join them on their morning walks, but Shane was always polite enough to extend the invitation. There had been a particularly late jam session the night before which Lauren had heard through her closed bedroom door, and Angel was still asleep. Chris and Chuck had apparently over-indulged on something more potent

97

than hard rock, for they lingered over the breakfast table drinking coffee through exaggerated groans and grimaces and looking generally miserable. Shane seemed to enjoy taunting them with his energy and early-morning cheer.

'I'll tell you, man,' Chris muttered at last, squinting at him through bloodshot eyes, 'this back-to-nature trip may be just the thing for you, but it's about to kill me. What kind of weirdo could actually enjoy walking at this hour of the morning?'

'What's killing you has nothing to do with nature,' Shane retorted goodnaturedly.

'Yeah, I know,' responded Chuck thickly behind a yawn. 'We need to mend our wicked ways.' And then he focused on Shane. 'Tell me something, man, when're you going to slide on down into all this sin and depravity with us where you belong? Whatever happened to you, anyway?'

Lauren sensed a very slight change come over Shane; he almost seemed uncomfortable. She had noticed that attitude often when he was in the company of the two men, he sometimes seemed nervous and ill at ease, and he always very carefully kept the topics of conversation on neutral ground. He did not mind discussing with them the technicalities of music and production, but whenever the conversation turned to the creative end of the business he always dropped out. Lauren knew he had been trying to avoid just such a personal question.

He dropped his eyes to his own coffee cup as he replied with a forced lightness, 'I like it just fine where I am.'

Chris made a derogatory sound. 'You've got to be kidding me! You like being a nobody? You like spending half your time in this godforsaken backwater watching the grass grow? I mean, it's nice for a vacation but, man, on the road is where it's at! What're you trying to pull?'

Shane lifted his eyes, but it was to Lauren and not the two men that he looked. In his eyes she saw the same sense of bleakness and isolation she herself had experienced so many times since her injury. Lauren herself had wanted to ask the same questions that Chris and Chuck were putting to him now, but not, perhaps, for the same reasons. She could relate to the frustration and loneliness Shane was now feeling even if she did not understand the reasons for it, because she had been there herself. Chuck and Chris, music people themselves, should have been expected to at least know some sympathy for Shane's position, to know what he had lost and to realise how sensitive a subject it had become. But no one at the table at that moment seemed to know what Shane was feeling except Lauren.

He looked at Chris, and then at Chuck, and he said softly, 'You guys just don't understand, do you? You're so wrapped up in the good times, in being on top and playing it for all it's worth, that you just ... don't understand.'

There was just a moment of silence, and Chris and Chuck were the ones who now looked confused and out of place. Then Shane reached for Lauren's hand, and smiled. 'Come on, Lauren, let's leave these two to their hangovers and get some fresh air.'

And for that brief moment as he wrapped his hand about hers Lauren felt a sort of silent communication with him, a sharing they had never experienced before. She knew how he felt.

But the episode started curiosity working within her anew. How difficult it must be for him to work so closely with music all day and not succumb to the urge to make his own. What adjustments had he had to make in order to take a back seat in a world that had once belonged to him? Weren't there volumes of music of his own stacked away somewhere, unsung, unrecorded, waiting for him to wake up and start living again?

One night as she helped Marie with the dinner dishes, she asked her about it.

'I don't believe Shane has written anything since his

last album,' Marie answered rather vaguely, rinsing glasses before she placed them in the dishwasher.

'Is it,' asked Lauren hesitantly, 'because of his wife's death?' It was still hard for her to think of Shane as having ever been married; it was harder still to admit to herself the possibility that all his inspiration had come from the woman he loved—and that, once that inspiration was gone, so was his music. Whenever she thought of his past she experienced a vague sort of hurt, because there were so many things tying him to a part of his life she could never share, and perhaps the strongest of these was a woman she had never known, and with whom she could not compete.

Marie responded cautiously, not looking at her, 'I imagine that's part of it.'

'What was she like?' asked Lauren cautiously. Perhaps if she could understand the woman who had once played such an important part in his life, she would somehow be able to better understand the man.

But Marie only answered, 'We never knew her. Why don't you ask Shane?'

Lauren gave an exaggerated pretence of horror. 'And get my head snapped off? No, thanks!'

Marie laughed, sponging off the counter tops. 'You wouldn't be the first. The damage is rarely permanent. Besides,' she added obscurely, 'I think he's past the snapping stage with you, now.'

Lauren glanced at her quickly, but Marie's face remained impassive. She wondered what changes, exactly, Marie had observed in their relationship, but she only commented, 'I don't know, it's hard to tell with him. You never know when he's going to turn on you.'

'Well, I can tell you this,' Marie answered. 'If you want anything from Shane, you have to push him for it. He's too insecure to volunteer information otherwise.'

Now Lauren stared at her. 'Insecure?'

But Marie chose not to elaborate. Instead, as she loosened the ties which held back the café curtains over the sink, she enquired, 'How are you two getting along, anyway?'

Lauren shrugged, thinking about that one moment of blinding sensuality in one another's arms upon a foggy hillside, and then trying not to think about it. It had meant nothing. A fantasy come to life for Lauren, an impulse satisfied for him. For in the past week, nothing—not a word, not a glance, not a touch—had in any way indicated to her that he even recalled the episode, much less that he had spent as many sleepless nights as she had, dreaming about it. 'We get along okay, I guess,' she answered. 'We seem to manage that just fine when we don't talk.'

Marie turned to look at her, untying the apron she had used for kitchen work, and suggested, 'I thought there might be something a little more serious going on.'

Lauren gave a startled laugh. 'What could be going on between Shane Holt and—and *me*?' The emphasis she put on the last word expressed more than she really meant to reveal about her feelings regarding the situation. Shane Holt was a superstar, and she was a nothing, and she was still, regrettably, suffering from a mild case of hero-worship.

'Lauren, that's ridiculous!' exclaimed Marie with a touch of asperity. 'Haven't you realised yet that Shane is every bit as human as you are—and in some ways, even more vulnerable? I thought surely as soon as you met him . . .'

'That's easy for you to say,' replied Lauren uncomfortably, turning to centre the vase of poppies on the breakfast nook, 'you've known him forever. And anyway,' she changed the subject quickly, 'the only thing I've ever wanted to know about him was his music, and he guards any mention of that like a state secret.' She knew that she was not being entirely truthful, but it was as much as she was willing to confide in Marie about her feelings for Shane right now. She looked at her, feeling more at ease now that the topic had moved on to more neutral ground. 'I can't help being curious, just like anyone else—and feeling that it's such a waste, the way he just left his music. But he won't talk to me about it.'

Marie's smile was sympathetic and understanding. 'Don't take it personally. You're not the only one who's concerned about Shane's career, and you're not the only one who's, as you put it, had their head snapped off when trying to help.' She slipped her arm about Lauren's waist as they started slowly through the dimly lit dining room and back towards the main part of the house. Her voice was lowered in confidence and concern as she went on, 'I'll tell you a secret. Shane is not a very good producer—no, I didn't mean to say that. In a business as competitive as this, I suppose he is good—but he'll never be great, you know what I mean? At best, all he can ever be is a shadow of Van, and I say that without any conceit, because he knows it as well as we do. Van has guided him along in the business, but Shane's heart isn't really in it. He's technically qualified, of course, but it takes so much more than knowing how to be really great at anything.' Her voice was sad as she added, 'Shane has that something else for composing . . . or at least he had. And I think the worst part is, he knows he'll never be anything but a second-rate producer, but he's content to settle for that.' She dropped her arm from about Lauren's waist and turned to extinguish the dining room light, then, as they stepped into the hallway, she looked at Lauren with a strange, gently encouraging smile. 'All of us who love Shane are trying to help him,' she told her quietly, 'but I think you have the best chance—if you would only go for it.'

And then, before Lauren could question or protest, she turned towards the sound of a sudden burst of laughter and the interminable video bleeps from down the hall and said brightly, 'Sounds like everyone's in the games room. Are you coming?'

But Lauren hung back, needing the time alone to sort out the new impressions and bits of half-information she had gained about Shane in the past half hour. 'In a minute,' she told Marie with a smile, and as Marie turned towards the games room, Lauren went in the opposite direction, towards the music room.

For once, it was deserted. She did not really know why she had come here, except that she always felt closer to Shane in this room. She wanted, more than anything at that moment, to close the door, put on one of his albums, and let him tell her with his music what he could not—or would not—with words. She even put her hand on one of the records, but then determinedly pushed the temptation away. She would not risk another scene like the last one . . . not yet.

There was an arrangement on the piano, and Lauren picked it up idly. She could read music well enough to tell it was something for Angel's band. The beat was fast rock, but the harmony was interesting, and she would have liked to have picked out the melody line, but the musical notation completely baffled her. She started to replace the music where she had found it, and Shane said behind her, 'Why don't you try it out?'

She turned, laughing a little to hide her surprise—and her nervousness, because she suddenly felt she didn't belong here. 'Are you kidding?' she responded and gestured around her towards the labyrinth of instruments and equipment. 'The only thing I recognise in here is the piano!'

He agreed, coming into the room. 'These days you don't need a degree in music to be a musician, but a degree in electronics.' He stood beside her near the piano, and smiled as he reached up and touched her hair. 'Do you realise this is the first time we've been alone all week?'

Her heart began to pound as she looked at him; she tried to subdue it. 'You've been busy,' she returned casually, moving a step away from him to trail her hand lightly over the casing of one of the keyboards.

'So have you,' he responded, watching her with a new note of reserve in his voice.

'Yes,' she agreed, 'but it was fun, wasn't it?' She tried to keep the conversation bright and neutral, wondering why he had followed her here, wondering if he had meant to provoke a reaction in her by reminding her of the last time they had been alone. If so, he had succeeded, because the warm memories flooded her, and with them, confusion and uncertainty. When she felt him touch her arm lightly, she jumped as though shocked, and then said quickly, to cover, 'What's this?'

For a moment he hesitated, and she tensed herself for a confrontation. But then, to her great relief, he apparently decided to follow her lead, and he stepped around her to switch on the synthesiser. 'One of the greatest contributions to twentieth-century music,' he replied. 'The only thing this particular little jewel doesn't do is sing, and I understand they have models now that do even that.' She watched his long fingers deftly moving switches, one hand on the keyboard and another on the console, and the strains of a fugue filled the air like magic. 'A little Bach,' he said as she drew in her breath in delight. 'How about some parlour music?' he suggested, and the instrument quickly became a clavichord beneath the competent ministrations of his fingers. 'Oh, hell, why go half way? Behold, Beethoven!' She covered her ears and gave a squeal of delighted amazement as the instrument, amplified to the maximum, grew into a full orchestra in the opening strains of the Ninth Symphony. The room throbbed and pulsed with it, she thrilled with it in every nerve of her body, and Shane, the musician, controlled it all with the fingers of two hands.

She filled with love and awe, watching him in such complete mastery of his art. It was where he belonged, where she had always imagined him to be, she felt almost reverent before him. And then he looked up, his easy grin breaking the spell as he left off the theme in the middle of a bar. 'It's a power machine,' he admitted, turning down the throbbing hum of the amplifiers. 'It can turn even a six-string guitar picker into a god.'

Lauren shook her head, still beaming with pleasure. 'You're not a six-string guitar picker.' Instead of being disappointed by his casual treatment of his talent, she was only impressed. This was his life, genius was only second nature to him, and she was honoured only to be able to witness it.

He shrugged it off and drew her forward with a hand lightly on her back. 'Come on, give it a try. You can get anything from a freight train to a pack of wolves out of this thing; it's fun to play with.'

'I'd rather have music,' she told him, relaxing in the fact that they were sharing easily and without constraint. 'Do some more.'

There was a relaxed twinkle in his eye as he enquired, 'What do I have to do to get a kiss from you?'

A half-breath caught in her throat, an unexpected colour pinkened her cheeks. Was he teasing her again? She decided she did not want to find out, not when so much about him was still in a turmoil in her mind, and she dropped her eyes demurely. 'Play,' she responded.

Shane bent his head to catch her expression, the spark in his eye now mischievous. 'That's not why I followed you in here,' he told her.

'Play,' she repeated sternly, her pulse racing.

'And when I do?'

'Then,' she told him, fighting back a smile, 'we'll talk about it.'

He laughed and turned back to the instrument. 'All right, what'll it be? Stravinsky? Sousa? How about a little McCartney, just to set the mood?'

His fingers were working the switches, touching the keys, filling the room with a familiar ballad. Watching it, loving the movements of his strong, slender fingers and the smoothness of his features as he concentrated on the music, the ease of mastery, she was moved beyond herself and into a part of him. She forgot for a moment all their differences and the strain of their relationship and remembered only that this was the man she had loved for ten years, who had filled her life with song and hope, and happiness flooded her just to be near him.

She rested her hand lightly upon the back of his neck. 'How about,' she suggested softly, 'a little Shane Holt?'

He stopped. She felt his muscles tense beneath her hand, and the room throbbed with silence. She stiffened and let her hand drop, horrified at her stupidity, for if he would not even discuss his music, why had she thought he might play it? She hadn't. She hadn't thought at all, she had simply let herself be carried away . . . she had ruined it all.

And then, saving the moment, a high, sweet voice from the corridor, picking up the melody where Shane had left off. He relaxed, turning back to the instrument and resuming the song as though nothing had interrupted it as Angel came into the room.

One by one, they floated into the room under the Pied Piper's spell of Shane's instrumentalisation—the drummer, picking up the soft tempo, the lead guitarist adding rhythm, Van fleshing it out with bass, Marie joining her voice in pretty harmony to Angel's. And Lauren slipped out unnoticed.

She made her way slowly upstairs, the music haunting her steps, reminding her with a vague aching in the centre of her chest that she did not belong there. With the musicians, Shane was relaxed and in his element, with her he was always holding back. She sighed as she pulled open the door of her closet and took out her nightclothes. What did she expect? It was her own clumsiness which kept pushing him away, causing him to constantly be on his guard against her. She knew the rules, and she seemed to be unable to avoid stumbling over them. But, she thought defensively, it was he who said we should get to know each other better, and even mentioned friendship . . . it was a careless statement, perhaps, obviously devoid of meaning, but it wasn't fair that he should lead her on and then keep turning her away.

Now, while everyone was involved downstairs, would

have been the perfect time to monopolise one of the three upstairs bathrooms for a long, relaxing bubble bath. But Lauren was still too keyed up for it, and she stepped out of her clothes, wrapping her hair in a towel, and into a quick, brisk shower.

The hot water left her skin flushed and pleasantly tingling, and she observed herself in the foggy mirrored tiles with some small satisfaction as she smoothed on a lightly scented lotion. She had gained a little weight—not much, but at least she did not look quite so emaciated any more. Her small breasts were more clearly defined now, her face looked fuller. Softness and symmetry was still marred by the sharp protrusion of collarbone and hipbones, and the scar of her knee was hideous, but she was improving. the past week of daily, arduous walking had completely eradicated the limp, except when she was very tired—or very nervous. For the first time, she was beginning to believe the doctor's forecast—that she would be able to live a perfectly normal life ... or almost normal.

Don't be an idiot, she told herself sternly as the familiar self-pity began to creep over her. You're alive, aren't you? You can walk, and see and hear and think ... so many worse things can have happened to you. Unconsciously, she was reflecting Van's words from his first visit in the hospital, and somehow, something of what Shane had said to her on the hilltop became intermingled with her own newly positive feelings about herself. Your body was made for more than dancing, she realised slowly, brushing her hair with long, firm strokes until it fell like silken honey across her bare shoulders. You should be proud it's healthy and relatively unscarred instead of burying yourself in sorrow over something that can't be changed.

She dressed, gave herself a brief, secretly encouraging smile in the mirror, scooped up her discarded clothes and left the bathroom feeling much better about everything than when she had entered.

The music was still going strong, and she hated to

close her door to block it out. She liked to think of
Shane as he had been in that moment before she had
ruined it all, his beautiful fingers working magic upon
the impersonal electronic box and his face softened with
the beauty of the music he created. But, almost
symbolically, she closed the door on the part of his
world in which she did not belong, and gave a little
gasp as she turned and saw Shane lounging on her bed.

'What are you doing here?' she exclaimed, startled. In
confusion she glanced towards the door, still half
believing that he was downstairs where she had last seen
him, for the music had been perfectly audible through
the noise of the shower and there had been no break.
'Who's playing the synthesiser? I thought——'

'The old quick change-over,' he answered with a
shrug, rising. 'It's one of the first tricks you learn on
stage, in case one of the performers is suddenly stricken
with cramp or stage fright or a heart attack—the show
must go on.' He came towards her slowly, a lazy light in
his eye sweeping her from head to foot. 'Oh, you look
beautiful!'

Lauren swallowed hard and turned quickly away to
put the bundle of clothes she carried on a chair. She
had a passion for sensuous nightclothes and satiny
underthings, and while her daytime wear was strictly
casual and practicable, she indulged her most frivolous
whims on personal clothing. One of her room-mates
had once exclaimed that half of Lauren's earnings must
go towards lingerie, and she was not far from wrong.
She was grateful that tonight's selection was not
particularly revealing—the chill of the house prevented
it—but she was aware that the coral and ivory lace-
trimmed peignoir she wore was one of her most
flattering garments, and she wondered what instinct
had prompted her to wear it tonight. The nightgown
was of a shimmery, satiny-feeling synthetic, full and
flowing from a sheer lace bodice which began just
above her nipples and gathered into a ruffle at the
throat. The matching robe was cut low to reveal the

lace nothingness of the bodice and fell in smooth, straight lines to the point just above her ankles where a deep ruffle of lace joined the nightgown. The material was some sort of brushed fleece, so light it gave the illusion of sheerness and outlined her body when she moved, so soft it was like cashmere beneath the fingers, inviting touching. And that, as Lauren straightened up, was exactly what Shane did.

His arms slipped about her from the back, his hands splayed across her abdomen, drawing her against his firm length and into the circle of his muscled arms. Automatically, as though he had pressed a button commanding adrenalin to flow and heart to pound, her blood began to course a fine flush over her body, her breathing became shallow, every nerve ending quickened in response to his touch. She tried to subdue the quivering which began with the sensuous motions of his fingers upon the material that covered her abdomen, and said, struggling for a normal tone, 'You never did tell me what you were doing here.'

He smiled, and turned her within the circle of his arms to face him. 'We had some unfinished business, I believe,' he responded, and lowered his face to hers.

His kiss was sure and soft, gentle but possessive, allowing no room for resistance on her part, or even the thought of it. And, as her arms curved automatically about his neck and her body swayed into the curve of his, resistance or protest was the last thing on Lauren's mind. Something quickened within him at her easy response—delight, or surprise, or simply instinct, she could not be sure—and his hands tightened upon her back, pressing her closer, molding her into his shape. His mouth explored her parted lips, teasing them in a slow, deliberate, maddeningly provocative dance of the senses. Her fingertips were hot as they brushed the back of his neck, tingling with the feather-softness of his hair, drifting down to tighten on his broad shoulders for support. His hands wandered downwards, feathering against the backs of her thighs, caressing her buttocks,

slowly massaging the satiny material of her nightgown
into her tingling skin. Her body grew weak and pliable
as his grew only stronger, more tense, yet with a
deliberately maintained restraint as he moved his hands
and his lips in an expert pattern of sensuality against
her body, exploring and savouring each sensation to the
fullest before moving on ... moulding her, weakening
her, leading, not pushing, her to the point of
vulnerability where she would no longer be able to
refuse him anything.

His lips left hers tingling and throbbing for more as
his hand lightly pushed back her hair, baring her ear to
the warm, moist explorations of his tongue. She
shivered and clung to him, bending her head backwards
with the course his lips traced upon the length of her
throat, soft kisses, the gentle pressure of teeth, the
delicate darting of a moist tongue ... The fleece robe
was suddenly too hot, she was burning with a flush and
perspiration filmed her skin; she wished he would take
it off. If her hands had not been so heavy she would
have done it herself, removing at least one of the
barriers which lay between them ... and, with that, a
small amount of reason filtered through.

Shane was a man of unquestioned experience and
innate sensuality; he most likely knew that no woman
could hold out against him for long. It was a game he
liked to play, nothing more, and if it ended the way he
wanted—the way he was making her want—he would
have forgotten about it as soon as he left her.

She turned her head away from the throbbing pressure
of his lips against her neck; she opened her eyes and
looked at him, placing unsteady hands flatly against his
chest, wedging distance between them. She said
deliberately, though in hardly more than a whisper,
'You're a very skilled lover, aren't you?'

He surprised her by accepting her signal to stop,
straightening up and moving his hands to rest lightly on
her waist. The smile in his eyes was gentle, though still
muted by the residue of smoky passion. 'Why do I get

the impression that was not a compliment?' he responded softly.

'Because ...' She tightened her hands against his chest, tried to stiffen her body, but she was still too much a part of him to move away. Still her pulses raced and her skin was flushed and her limbs heavy, she wanted only to sink mindlessly into his embrace again. But she steeled herself. 'Because,' she told him steadily, 'there's more to making love than just technical skill ... just like there's more to producing records than just knowing how.'

She tensed herself for the coldness, for the anger, for the painful withdrawal. But the gentle light in his eyes did not fade, he registered no surprise. The corners of his lips deepened with a small, slightly mocking smile as he returned lightly, 'Insults, from my one and only remaining loyal fan? I'm hurt!' But he did not look hurt. He looked patient, vaguely amused, tender. He reached up gently to stroke her hair, adding, 'Sounds as though you've been talking to Marie ... about record producing, I hope, and not about lovemaking techniques!'

Lauren nodded, surprised by his casual acceptance of the fact. But hadn't Marie told her he held no illusions about himself as a producer? She was glad, because she really had not wanted to insult him ... or hurt him. She had only wanted to break the mood.

But in that she had not quite succeeded. She dropped her hands from his chest, feeling foolish for letting him hold her so intimately when she was desperately trying to avoid intimacy with banal conversation. But in this he refused to take the hint. His hands remained steady on her waist, the strength of his thighs hard against hers, the lazy light of lingering sensuality still in his eyes. 'Are you trying to tell me,' he asked softly, winding a strand of her hair about his finger, 'that sex without love is meaningless? Or are you saying that you don't find me quite as desirable as you thought you would?'

She took a step backwards. Deliberately, she closed her hands about his wrists and released their hold on her waist. She said, quite evenly, 'I'm trying to tell you that I'm not a big enough fan to go to bed with you. So if that's what you're looking for, go search out one of your old groupies. I told you before, I'm not one of them.'

And it was those words, unplanned and unrehearsed, which had the effect of abruptly breaking the spell. Shane stiffened, he dropped his eyes briefly. When he looked at her again his expression was completely unreadable . . . was it shock, disappointment, a mortally wounded ego? He must have thought it would be so easy, she thought in rising anger, to seduce the child who had been following him around like a desperate puppy, hanging on his every word, exhibiting in her every action unmitigated adoration . . . he would satisfy an appetite while subtly mocking her, and how disappointed he must be to be discovered! And just as it was all beginning to make horrible, twisted sense, his words shattered her rationale, leaving her both relieved and confused.

'If and when you do go to bed with me,' he said in a low voice, 'it will not be for that reason. I'll make damn sure of it.' There was a quiet sort of fury in his eyes, now stripped completely of the bright gleam of passion, and a bitter disappointment. 'And if you think I'm any more interested in casual sex than you are, you're wrong. I've had enough of that to last a lifetime, and I thought it might be different with us . . . I guess I was wrong.'

He turned and started towards the door, and Lauren watched him in shock and confusion, hugging her arms against a sudden chill the absence of him had left. Why was she always misjudging him? Why did she always manage to say just the right thing to hurt and anger him . . . when the last thing in the world she wanted to do was hurt him? He opened the door, and she wanted to call him back, to apologise

and to comfort him, and to try to make things right
between them again.

And then, just when she thought it was too late, he
closed the door, turning slowly and leaning against it.
'Ah, hell,' he muttered softly, 'what am I doing?' The
expression on his face was contrite, behind the tight,
self-mocking smile there was gentle pleading in his eyes.
'I can't go back down there,' he admitted simply. 'If I
promise not to throw you on the bed and rip off all
your clothes, can I stay?'

She caught her breath in pure astonishment. 'But—
why?'

'For the same reason I came up here in the first
place,' he answered. 'To get away from all that noise
and just be alone with you in a quiet place for a while.'

He came across the room towards her, seeking her
permission to stay. 'We could talk,' he suggested. 'Or if
you don't want to, just sit here and enjoy the solitude
for a while. I promise I won't touch you.'

In total confusion, and because he was waiting for an
answer, Lauren noded. 'O-okay,' she agreed. And, still
weak from his overpowering sensuality and the abrupt
about-face, she sank nervously to the edge of the bed,
anxiety and curiosity about what lay ahead moving her
to new alertness.

True to his word, Shane did not approach her, but
took the only other available sitting surface, the chair
arranged near the window, a few feet from the bed.
Carefully removing Lauren's clothes to the dresser top,
he arranged himself comfortably in the chair, long legs
crossed at the ankles hands linked across his chest. And
he said nothing.

'Well,' she invited after a moment, clasping her hands
in her lap and trying to look as casual as he did, 'what
do you want to talk about?'

His grin was completely disarming, and he responded,
'Sex.'

She laughed, the tension and the nervousness draining
away into the easy twinkle in his eyes. 'Be serious!'

'I am serious,' he assured her. 'I have just one final word to say on the subject, and then we'll move on to safer ground. Don't ever criticise a man's technique, Lauren.' he advised, and she could not tell whether the sobriety in his tone was real or assumed. 'It does strange things to the libido, and has a positively devastating effect on the ego.'

'I—I wasn't criticising,' she said, glancing at him and trying futilely to subdue a blush. She was not sure whether or not he was teasing, but she could not take the chance of letting him think she objected to his lovemaking—or anything he did. 'I—I liked it, actually,' she confessed, and his smile was gentle and encouraging.

'I'm glad,' he responded, and now there was no doubt that he was serious, 'because I only wanted to give you pleasure.' His eyes, steady and unreserved, held her with as much force as his hands had ever done, and the softness of his voice stroked her like a caress. The short distance between them was suddenly filled with sensuality, soft, inundating, magnetic. 'You bring out that characteristic in me,' he went on in a voice as smooth as silk, as mesmerising as a melody. 'The need to give pleasure, to make you happy . . . I think because there seems to be so little of either in your life right now, and because I don't think I've ever known anyone who needed to feel good more than you do. I just want to do that for you.'

Lauren nodded, colour heightening, and said softly, 'You do.'

The atmosphere surrounding them had become subtly erotic, and, as aware of it as she was, Shane abruptly changed the subject. 'And now on to safer ground. How have you been this past week?'

She laughed a little, grateful for his command of the situation and the sense with which he handled it. 'Okay,' she answered. 'How about you?'

'Lonely,' he replied immediately, and she was startled.

'How can that be?' she demanded. 'You've been so busy, always with people . . .'

He dismissed it with a negligent turn of his wrist. 'Lonely in a crowd, isolated . . . it's one of the things I hate most about the music business. There's no time to relax and be yourself.'

Her smile was puzzled, tentative. 'Do you ever do that?'

'Sometimes,' he responded cautiously, 'with some people.'

'But not with me,' she added automatically, then glanced at him quickly, afraid she had overstepped the bounds of casual conversation.

But his face registered no sign of offence taken. 'I want to,' he told her. 'Sometimes I think I could, sometimes I even try. But you always push me away.'

She shook her head firmly, recognising a mixed truth in what he said. Sometimes, through her clumsiness or uncertainty, she did push him away, accidently or deliberately—but it was mostly the defences he built which kept her at a distance. For the first time, their interchange had moved on to a new level of openness and honesty, and she was determined to pursue it. 'You won't let me get close enough to push you away,' she told him. 'You're always on the defensive. The other day you said we should get to know each other better, but you won't give me a chance.'

In his eyes was a reluctant admission that she was right, but he tried to dismiss it lightly with, 'It's probably just as well. If you knew the real me, you probably wouldn't like it.'

She refused to be deterred. 'You won't let me find out,' she told him evenly. 'Every time I ask you a personal question or talk to you about your music, or . . .' she glanced at him swiftly, 'play one of your records, you get mad, or freeze up.'

For a moment he was silent, but his eyes did not leave hers. And then he said seriously, 'In the first place, my music has nothing to do with what I really am. If that's all you want to know about me—if that's all I'm worth to you—then read my album covers. But,' he added on a more pleasant note, 'in the interest of getting to know each other better, ask me a personal question—or two or three. I promise to answer them as well as I can without getting mad or freezing up ... providing I get the same privilege with your personal life when you're finished.'

She hesitated, then accepted his terms. 'All right,' she agreed cautiously. 'We'll start with something simple. Tell me about your family.'

'That's easy,' he answered, settling back in the chair. 'It's all a matter of public record. My father is vice-president of an international corporation, they're stationed in Japan now, I think.' At her look of surprise, he admitted, 'That's right, I really don't know. I haven't heard from them in a couple of years. The other night,' he added, looking at her with a strange expression, 'when you mentioned your parents, even though you really didn't say anything much about them at all, there was this look in your eyes ... of love, and happy memories. I was jealous.' Lauren's expression softened with amazement—both for the nature of the confession, and the ease with which he related it. Perhaps it was true that he had really wanted to share himself with her, but she had never given him a chance.

'We were never a close family,' he went on. 'My brothers—there are three of us—keep up some, but not like we should. My older brother is in computers and his company transfers him so often that I usually don't get his forwarding address until he's already someplace else. My younger brother got into some religious movement a few years ago and may as well have dropped off the face of the earth as far as the family is concerned. Of course, we were all abysmal failures in my parents' eyes. They raised us to be scholars, leaders, and corporate giants. My oldest brother has come closest to fulfilling their expectations, but he's forty years old and hasn't made vice-president yet, and they can't forgive him for that. As far as my youngest brother and myself are concerned—well, I don't know for sure, but I think we've been disinherited.' He shrugged. 'I don't guess I can really blame them.'

'How sad,' Lauren said softly.

'I suppose so,' he agreed, 'to someone who's known a real family. I never had it, so I never missed it.'

She hesitated, then screwed up her courage to broach a more sensitive subject. 'Would it upset you,' she ventured, 'to talk about your wife?'

He looked at her for a moment, seemed to recall his promise to answer her questions while at the same moment debating whether her company or his privacy was the most valuable to him at that point. She was relieved when he smiled a little, as though to reassure her, and answered, 'No, it won't upset me.' But then he shifted his gaze, his eyes turned inward, skimming across uncertainties and unresolved conflicts within himself, looking slightly puzzled and unsure. Lauren was not certain whether he was trying to remember, or trying to forget. 'Emily was ... a nice girl,' he said at last. 'Bright and bubbly and fun to be with. She was a ski instructor,' he added, glancing at her, and Lauren understood why skiing had become a sensitive subject with him—and perhaps why he so diligently avoided the snow now, which would always remind him of a lost happiness. Her heart ached, but she was not certain whether it was for him, or herself. 'We were in love,' he went on slowly, thoughtfully, 'for a while, and then it just sort of—faded away, like a cheap photograph that's been left in the sun. She didn't want to get married, but I suppose I thought having a wife, someone waiting at home for me when I was on the road, would give a focal point to my life, an anchor. Of course it's stupid to try to be married in the profession I was in. I don't know, maybe if I had been home, maybe if she'd tried harder to make me settle down, we could have salvaged something out of what we once had . . . but the marriage went steadily downhill from day one.'

There was suffering in his eyes and Lauren experienced with him all the things he had left unsaid, all the pain, the regret, the guilt . . . She wanted to draw him into her arms and comfort him, to tell him to put the past behind and try to forget what had gone before . . . she wanted to make him forget, if she could.

But, forcefully, Shane dragged himself from the dark mood and looked up at her, abruptly changing the subject. 'Now it's my turn,' he announced. 'Do you always wear those frilly nightgowns to bed, or do you sometimes sleep in the nude? And if you do sleep in nightgowns, do you wear anything at all beneath them? What is it that makes your skin taste like flowers? Do you——'

She laughed, bringing up her hands to ward off his questions and hide her bright cheeks and sparkling eyes. 'Unfair! You didn't warn me you meant *personal*!'

'I answered yours,' he returned, his expression bland behind madly dancing eyes. 'You answer mine.'

She brought her hands down and folded them beneath her chin, meeting his challenge with laughter in her eyes and a demure smile on her lips. 'Yes, no, and body lotion,' she replied, and his eyes snapped with approval and amusement.

'This is kind of fun,' he admitted. 'Shall we go on?'

'I think we've gotten personal enough for one evening,' she returned grimly, straightening the folds of her robe about her knees.

'It's just as well,' he agreed easily. 'Too much stimulating conversation this late at night can't be good for the health.'

'Is that right?' she laughed.

He stood and extended his hands to her, drawing her to her feet. 'That's right,' he told her, his eyes as warm as his fingers upon hers. 'Leading directly to too many cold showers, which, as we all know, are a primary cause of pneumonia.' She laughed, and he brushed her lips very lightly with a kiss. 'I'd better go,' he told her his eyes twinkling, 'before I catch pneumonia.' And he kissed her again, more firmly. When he looked at her all signs of teasing were gone, and he said simply, 'It's been good being with you tonight, Lauren. Thanks for offering me shelter.'

She smiled. 'Any time,' she answered.

'Careful,' he warned, touching her nose playfully. 'I might just take you up on that!'

Her smile followed him across the room. 'Goodnight, Shane,' she said.

He turned at the door, his eyes warm and reluctant. 'Goodnight, Lauren.' And he added gently, 'Sleep well.'

The next day dawned cold and rainy, and the morning walk was postponed. It was just as well, because the house was in a flurry getting Angel's group ready for the return trip to the airport. About mid-morning, the rain stopped, clearing abruptly into patches of sunshine and brilliant flashes of blue between banks of fast-moving, charcoal-shaded clouds. Lauren seized the opportunity to escape from the clutter and the frantic conversation of last-minute catching up and reluctant goodbyes, and stepped out into the cool air of the patio.

Within moments, she heard the door close again softly behind her, and when she turned she was surprised to see it was Angel who joined her. She smiled to Lauren and came over to her, taking a deep breath of the cool, wet air and at the same time drawing a cigarette from the deep pocket of her hip-length suede vest. 'Don't tell on me,' she said with an endearing grin as she brought the cigarette to her mouth and reached for her lighter. 'I'm not supposed to, you know, and I feel like a ten-year-old every time I sneak away to have a smoke.'

Lauren assured her her confidence was well placed, and she noticed Angel's hands were shaking badly as she lit the cigarette. She couldn't help staring, and Angel noticed with a nervous laugh as she drew deeply on the cigarette and replaced the lighter in her pocket. 'Don't let the shakes bother you,' she said, 'I'm not having a nicotine fit. My nerves are shot, that's all; it's a professional hazard.' Her restless eyes wandered over the turbulent skyline briefly, jerkily, as she once again inhaled the smoke and added, 'Shane had the right idea. He got out just in time.'

Lauren did not know what to say. She smiled politely and shifted her gaze to the misty mountains in the distance. She could feel the other woman's gaze, however, and when she glanced that way again Angel was looking at her with a curious smile on her face, her arms crossed over her chest against the chill, the cigarette poised lightly between two fingers. And she said, 'We never got a chance to know one another.' She laughed a little. 'I travel in a portable zoo, as I guess you noticed, and there's never any time for anything.' Then she added unexpectedly, 'You're Shane's girl, aren't you?'

Lauren was startled. 'Did—he tell you that?'

Angel shook her head, scattering ash to the ground with a few quick taps of her index finger. Her smile was secretive and affectionate. 'He didn't have to. You get to know a person well enough, and you pick up on these things.'

Shane's girl. The sound of it was thrilling, a little overwhelming, and, of course, completely exaggerated. Lauren asked, 'How long have you known him?'

'Oh, forever.' Angel tilted her head back to the breeze and drew deeply again on the cigarette. The wind carried the smoke over her head in a crooked angular stream. Her expression grew thoughtful, almost troubled, as she gazed beyond Lauren at the mountains and said, 'I owe him my life, I guess. Oh, he'd hate it if he ever heard me say that, but I don't know what else you'd call it.'

Lauren stared at her. 'I don't understand. What did he——'

Angel shrugged a little, embarrassed. 'It's a real

sordid story, and when you've been there you don't
want to talk about it. He just picked me up out of the
gutter when I was sinking fast, and turned me around
without even trying.' She tried to make it all sound very
casual, but Lauren could tell there was a deeply
protected emotion behind the story. 'When I thought I
couldn't make it, all I had to do was look at him to
know I could . . .' And then she looked at Lauren,
embarrassed again, as though suddenly realising she
was talking to a complete stranger. 'Well, anyway,' she
added on a brighter note, 'I'm sorry I didn't get to
know you better. I know Shane thinks a lot of you.' She
turned her head towards a call from inside the house,
quickly grinding out the cigarette beneath her shoe.
'Sounds like the last boarding call; I'd better get a move
on.'

   She started back inside, then turned back to Lauren,
a strange mixture of light warning and tender affection
on her face. 'Shane is very, very special,' she said softly.
'You be good to him, you hear?'

   Lauren could not help smiling, though rather
uncertainly, in return.

   Strange, she thought, and wandered off the patio on
to the soggy ground. A bare, wet bush brushed coldly
against her jeaned leg and she stroked its stubbly
branches absently. She wondered again what Angel's
relationship with Shane was. Protective, affectionate,
but more sisterly than lover-like. She supposed Shane
must have done her a favour at some time, something
which had saved or changed her career, and she was
eternally grateful. Well, that came as no surprise to
Lauren. The man she knew through his music was
generous, thoughtful, and cared deeply for the welfare
of others. And what about the man she had recently
come to know as separate from the musician? Not so
different, she reflected with some slow surprise.
Perceptive, sensitive, calmly observant . . . most of the
time. Often tender, unexpectedly sensuous, inexplicably
haunted . . . and by more, it seemed, than lingering grief

for the death of his family. Given to startling bursts of temper and irrationality ... Lauren shook her head wearily as she went back inside. How was she supposed to understand him when she couldn't even understand herself most of the time?

Silence lay over the house when she entered, unexpected and welcome. Like a sudden summer storm, they had burst upon the scene in a cacophony of colour and sound, then departed as abruptly as they had arrived, leaving the air refreshed and renewed and ... peaceful. Unconsciously, Lauren breathed a sigh of relief as she poured herself a cup of coffee, then, placing it on the breakfast table, went into the living room to find a magazine. Marie had left a plate of Danish pastries on the table, and Lauren intended to enjoy a leisurely, quiet mid-morning snack.

As she rifled through the magazine collection on the bookshelf—mostly music and entertainment publications—Lauren's eyes fell upon a heavy, over-stuffed scrapbook. Opening it, she discovered it was filled with clippings and little-known highlights about some of Van's famous protégés and, her interest immediately captured, she took it back to the kitchen with her.

She settled into a corner of the breakfast booth, sipping her coffee and nibbling on a Danish pastry, looking through the pages and idly wondering if Marie—for such meticulous work definitely bore the mark of Marie's hand—had included anything about Shane. Lauren did not read music magazines (as a matter of fact, the only time she even read *Variety* was when she was out of work), and she found these clippings, about some of her favourite performers fascinating. She soon became engrossed in the private philosophies of the stars, the unexpected beginnings, the incredible behind-the-scenes endeavours that went into the making of a hit record.

Then she turned a page, and stopped. There, filling two lengths of heavy black paper, Marie had lovingly placed every clipping, every notice, every review of every musical Lauren had ever danced in. Even if her name was not mentioned (which was often) Marie had saved the notice, writing on the side, 'Lauren—May, 1979' or 'Lauren, Chicago, '78—marvelous!' Tears of love and gratitude filled her eyes. Either Marie or Van had attended every opening in which she danced, ready with witty criticism or raving approval, and for the first time Lauren was struck by how fortunate she was to be so loved, so cared for.

As she looked at those clippings, familiar names and familiar places leaped into three dimensional life before her eyes—the hot lights, the smell of greasepaint and perspiration, the dusty boards, music swelling into the thunder of applause ... She could taste it, she could breathe it, she could feel strong hands about her waist lifting her high above the world in a triumphant turn, she could feel muscles straining in an ecstatic *jeté*, the lines of her body moulded by the music and buoying her, for that one brief moment before her feet touched ground again, into the realms of immortality. And, uncontrollably, the flood of memories dissolved into tears, slow, sluggish, mournful tears which moistened her lips and splashed into her coffee, entirely unexpected, completely unpreventable.

She felt a gentle hand upon her shoulder, then Shane was sliding into the booth beside her, drawing her head on to his chest, simply holding her, not saying a word. She felt foolish, but the tenderness of the gesture only increased the flow of tears. She wanted to lie against his chest and have him hold her for ever, to feel the softness of his shirt against her cheek and the heat of his body beneath, to sob all her heartbreak and disappointment into his strength, where it would be absorbed and disappear. But she tried to push away, scrubbing futilely at her wet face with the back of her hand and managed thickly, 'Silly! I'm—getting your shirt all wet.'

'I won't melt,' he assured her calmly, and gently drew her back to the warm, solid wall of his chest. His voice

was like music. 'Everyone is entitled to one long look
back and one good cry. You go ahead and have yours.'

She reached her arm up, her fingers curling against
his shoulder, and felt his lips lightly brush her hair as
the tears came, easy, without restraint, cleansing and
refreshing. You're here for me, she thought distantly,
just as you've always been ... comforting me,
encouraging me, holding me in a part of you and giving
me hope ... just as you've always done.

'Since I was a child,' she began softly, 'it's all I ever
wanted to do. The music was in my blood, the theatre
was born into me. The bit parts, the scratchings and
clawing for jobs, the bad reviews and the early closings
... I didn't mind any of it. It was what I *did*. Oh, I had
dreams of being a star, like everyone else, but it didn't
matter so much as long as I was dancing ...' She closed
her eyes against a fresh wash of warm tears, but Shane's
hand stroked her hair silently and it was easier to talk
after a moment. 'The show I was in—this last show—it
opened on Broadway last month. I should have been
there. I would have been there, only ...' her voice
almost broke. 'Oh, Shane, it was so stupid, so unfair! I
just *fell*. Right at the end of the performance in the
second week of off-Broadway openings ... I was tired,
I should have been more careful ...' Her fist tightened
against his shoulder as she struggled with the
nightmarish memory. 'Everyone falls, it's no big deal,
but—the minute I hit the boards I knew ...' Her voice
fell to a whisper. 'I knew.' It was a moment before she
could go on, and then it was in a voice dull with shock
and an overload of emotions. 'The doctors—they did
their best, but the knee had been injured too many
times before and ... there just wasn't much left to
patch together, I guess. They kept telling me I should
feel lucky that I would be able to walk and lead a
normal life ... but I didn't feel very lucky.' Then she
could do nothing but let the tears come, to lie against
him and let the agony of failure and disappointment
flood her. It was a long time before she could manage,

with a shaky breath, 'Oh, Shane! Does it ever get better?'

'No,' he answered quietly. 'But after a while, it comes less often. After a while, you learn to bear it.'

And somehow, sharing the pain eased the terrible hurt inside her, the yearning for what was so real she could almost touch it, yet so far away it would never be hers again. Because Shane, of all the people in the world, knew what she had lost. He had been there before her and now without even trying, was making the way easier for her, just as he had always done.

The morning shifted in patterns of light and shade as clouds scuttled across the high window over the breakfast nook, and Lauren rested against him, drawing strength from him, feeling the growing process begin within her in ways as subtle as the silence, as impossible to define as the shadows which moved across them . . . simply knowing that, because it was inevitable, she would learn to deal with her loss, and because the time had come, she could find a way to move on in her life. Feeling warm, protected, and good about herself. Feeling loved.

At last she stirred, and reached for a paper napkin to dry her face. She ventured a glance at Shane, and a little smile. He responded by stroking her hair, once, and saying seriously, 'You know this is the worst place in the world for you to be right now, don't you?'

She was startled, puzzled. 'What——'

'In Colorado,' he explained, 'with winter coming on. Under Van's protection. Isolated, with too much time to think. You need to be in New York, looking for work, getting your life back together.'

She shook her head slowly, balling up the damp napkin. 'I—don't think I'm ready for that yet.' Again, the pain began to swell. 'Performing was my *life*,' she said intensely, unconsciously tightening her hands into double fists. 'I never wanted anything else, not ever. It was more than just a job—like being a secretary or an accountant—it was a gift, a calling, it made me feel . . .

special.' She looked at him. 'Chosen. When I was dancing . . .' Now her eyes took on a dreamy look, an anxious look not too far from wistfulness. 'It was as though, for a time, I could live out every fantasy man has ever had and share them. I was in another world, I was—invincible, immortal, I could bring dreams to life, there was nothing I couldn't do.' Her eyes were shining now as she focused on him. 'And there's a kind of magic to the theatre, knowing that you hold the fates of hundreds of people in your hand for two hours out of their lives . . . *you*, all alone on that stage, are going to manipulate them, make them laugh when you want to and cry when you want them to and determine whether they leave you happy or sad or—disappointed. Oh, it's scary. But it's compulsive. And when it all works just right, when the rapport is there, when they love you . . .' She broke off, recalling suddenly to whom she was speaking, and her smile was slightly embarrassed, but mostly grateful. Because he really did understand. 'But I don't have to tell you. You know what it's like.'

He had been watching her with an intense, very absorbed expression, but now his features relaxed slowly into negligence; he lifted one eyebrow slightly. 'No,' he admitted, and he got up from the table. 'I hated performing.'

For a moment Lauren was actually speechless. She watched him cross the room towards the coffeepot, and her head was reeling with a dozen impressions, none of them concerning herself. Abruptly, she forgot her own needs and yearnings in the collage of memories of his one performance she had witnessed . . . The composure, the earnestness, the strength with which he reached out and captured the audience, the magic he worked from the stage. 'But——' She started to say, 'you were so good at it!', but that was only stating the obvious. She changed it to simply, 'Why?'

Shane refilled her cup and his own, answering, 'It was life on the road, mostly. Missed meals, no sleep, forgetting what city you're in and sometimes what state

... loneliness, stage fright, too many empty rooms and empty faces ...' He glanced at her, and a slightly embarrassed smile touched his face as they both realised at once that he was quoting from one of his songs. He left the coffee pot on the table and went to the refrigerator for cream. 'It wasn't for me,' he finished, with his back to her. 'I couldn't handle it.'

But Lauren wondered if the real reason was not the fact that he blamed the rigours of performing for the failure of his marriage, and that he was using guilt as an excuse for doing what he was meant to do ... as a sort of punishment. She asked softly, watching him, 'Why did you stop writing?'

His eyes were lowered as he poured a measure of cream into his cup; she thought he would not answer. Then, straightening up to return the cream to the refrigerator, he said simply, 'I don't know where all the melodies went.'

'Have you even tried?'

She felt his tension as he returned to the table. His eyes were veiled and she could sense imminent withdrawal, perhaps, even anger. But she remembered Marie's advice—that if you wanted anything from Shane, you had to push. And she wanted to put an end to the reserve he held against her, the barriers he kept forcing between them. She was willing to push for it.

To her relief, he appeared in the mood to make some sort of compromise. He only replied lightly, 'You ask too damn many questions, you know that?' And he took his coffee over to the window, turning there to look at her. His expression was relaxed, but there was wariness in his eyes. Lauren remained firm, demanding an answer with her silence, and at last he admitted, 'No, I haven't tried. I haven't wanted to.'

'But *why*?' she insisted. 'Shane, your career was just at its peak. You were a top recording star, you didn't *have* to leave it all. How could you turn your back on it?'

He sipped his coffee calmly, but she could tell he was

forcefully restraining emotion. 'In the first place,' he replied patiently, 'I was hardly a top recording star. As a matter of fact, one very good reason I stopped recording was because I lost my contract.'

She stared at him. She knew enough from Van to realise that studios did not release their artists without a very good reason—greed on the part of the performer being the most common. She could not believe that Shane had ever been greedy, and she knew his last album had been his biggest seller, and all she could manage was, 'How?'

He looked at her for a moment as though debating whether or not to answer. When he did speak there was an odd tone to his voice, almost a challenge, and she knew he was very near the end of his patience. 'You noticed, no doubt,' he said drily, pretending casualness as he sipped from his cup, 'that my nose has been broken. It happened in a bar-room brawl with two of the studio's top executives and my producer. I don't remember much about it, but they tell me I acted like I was out to kill somebody. I was lucky nobody brought charges, I guess, but the studio didn't need too many more reasons to get rid of me.'

He was watching her closely for a reaction, his eyes narrowed as though daring her to challenge his story. Lauren's reaction was utter astonishment; it was all she could do to keep from bursting into laughter. Shane Holt, attacking three men in physical battle? It was absurd. This was the gentle dreamer, the weaver of magic, the poet and the scholar. That he would ever do such a thing was beyond all imagination, and she wondered why he had told it for the truth.

She said, meeting his eyes evenly, 'I don't believe you.'

His eyes grew hard. He replied briefly, 'I know you don't.' And he drained his coffee cup.

She continued easily, even though her heart was pounding with the sudden increased tension in the room, 'Anyway, you could have gone to another studio, gotten a better contract. That's no reason.'

'Oh, for Pete's sake, Lauren,' he burst out impatiently, 'let it go, will you?' He strode across the room to place his cup on the counter, and in the few minutes his back was turned to her he seemed to struggle to regain control. In a moment he said, more calmly, 'Look, I was just another top-forties artist, no more. I never had a number one hit and I never would have. I never sold a million copies of anything. I never won an award. I have a mediocre voice with a one-octave range, I play a passable guitar and pretty fair keyboards, but beyond that I could be anybody on the street.' Now he turned and looked at her. 'No one misses my music,' he told her flatly. 'There are a dozen new ones just like me hitting the charts every month. There was nothing special about my music, it didn't irrevocably alter history or change anyone's life. It——'

'It changed my life,' Lauren interrupted softly.

The moment between them was poignant; it throbbed across the distance between them with challenge and meaning. But beyond the softening flicker of surprise in his eye was caution, denial, and sadness. And there was heaviness in his voice as well as wariness in his face as he said, 'That's all I mean to you, isn't it? That's all you see in me—what I was, or what you thought I was. Just words and music.'

'No,' she insisted earnestly, rising. 'It's what you *are*, what you could be again.' She reached him; she placed her hand lightly on his arm. 'Shane, I know you. I know you couldn't just walk away from your gift, any more than I could from mine. And I care about that, not only because of what you've taken from all of us who loved your music, but because of what it's doing to you. Don't you see——'

'Damn it, Lauren, you don't know me!' he exploded. He jerked his arm away abruptly and turned to grip the kitchen counter, his back stiff. 'You don't know me and you never will, and how dare you presume to judge me! Can't you get it through your head that I don't want your help and I don't need your interference? It's none of your business!'

She fell back, hurt as though physically struck, aching and confused. The moment she had thought to capture between them had shattered like glass, too fragile to withstand the impact of the violent emotions she had roused. She wondered if it would ever be repaired, and the worst of the pain was that she did not think so.

Shane said roughly, not looking at her, 'Why the hell don't you get your own life straightened out before you start interfering in mine?'

For a long moment, silence throbbed between them, aching and cold. Lauren could see the anger and the struggle within him in the squared lines of his back, his tensely hunched shoulders. She could hear it in the soft rush of his breath. But if he regretted any of what he had said, he would not let her know, and the yearning and sorrow within her gradually began to build into something more—a stubbornness to match his own.

At last she said quietly, lifting her chin a fraction and squaring her shoulders, 'Thanks. I think I will.'

And she turned and left the room.

CHAPTER SEVEN

FOR the next two weeks Lauren and Shane maintained their distance carefully, almost warily. On fair mornings they walked, he held her hand and they talked sporadically, always about neutral subjects. Occasionally she would glance up during the course of her day and find him watching her, and sometimes the expression in his eyes was patiently amused, other times it was serious, as though he were on the point of an apology or a personal discussion about the unhappy changes in their relationship. Lauren always thwarted any such overtures, however, and he fell back without resistance, waiting.

She was guarding her emotions much more carefully these days. Foolishly, she had allowed herself to forget who Shane was, and who she was. She had tried to bring the fantasy to life, and to get closer to him than he would allow, and that had been a mistake. As he had pointed out, she had more pressing things to concern her at this point than what he chose to do with his life—primarily, what she was going to do with her own.

She launched on a determined programme of self-improvement. One day while shopping with Marie she secretly purchased a leotard and fell into the morning ritual of limbering, warm-up, and yoga exercises which had been a part of her life for so many years. The results surprised her, not only in improved muscle tone and a healthier appearance, but in increased energy and self-confidence. She was doing this for herself, not because she had to or expected approval from anyone, but simply because she cared about herself for the first time since the accident. She knew she would never dance again, she had accepted that and was not maintaining false hope or encouraging fantasies in that

131

direction. But all her life she had been in peak physical condition, and she wondered now for the first time if letting herself go in those first months after the accident had not contributed more than she realised to the depression.

During one four-day weekend Van had the house filled with guests again, and while Lauren found it much easier to mingle and get to know the party, it was Shane who generally found an excuse to be otherwise occupied. Constantly, executives and technicians from Van's Denver studio were wandering in and out, and Lauren found the exposure to new people stimulating and exciting. She was beginning to feel more like herself. Shane accompanied Van and some of his colleagues on a three-day fishing trip, and other than that, he kept mostly to himself . . . and Lauren had the feeling that, while all of these welcome, growing changes were taking place within her, Shane was quietly observing her, saying nothing, giving her space.

She found herself sleeping less, rising earlier, just as she had been accustomed to doing all her life. Often she was awake before anyone else, and had an hour or so alone in the kitchen with a cup of coffee, watching the sun rise and feeling peaceful. But one morning, though, she came downstairs to the aroma of coffee, and found Shane in the kitchen before her, standing at the window. His voice floated softly across the dimly lit room to her; he was facing the window and completely unaware of her entrance.

'Hello, bird,' he said. 'You're looking good this morning. What are you still doing here this time of year, anyway?'

Lauren brought her hand to her mouth to cover a delighted smile as the object of his address, a small brown bird perched on the sill, cocked his head intelligently and gave a few staccato chirps.

'Hmm,' replied Shane thoughtfully. 'I know what you mean. Well, life is rough all over, isn't it?'

The bird, perhaps suddenly noticing Lauren's

presence, chirped again and flew away. Shane turned and saw her, but his grin was more surprised than embarrassed. 'Aha,' he said, coming over to her. 'Now you know my fault. I talk to animals.'

She lifted an eyebrow in mock amazement, thoroughly delighted with the scene she had just witnessed. 'Your fault? You mean you only have one?'

'I have,' he returned, filling a cup for her and freshening his own coffee, 'hundreds. But only one of them makes itself manifest at this hour of the morning.'

He was wearing jeans and a black sweatshirt, his hair was slightly tousled and his feet were bare. He looked rumpled, warm, and embraceable. His smile was sleepy as he handed her cup to her, and Lauren found herself returning the smile without restraint. 'In other words,' she told him, 'you're only crazy in the morning.'

'In other words,' he responded, 'I'm a perfect doll in the mornings. Kind to children, animals, and pretty young things in blue satin robes.' She acknowledged the compliment by unconsciously straightening the lace on her collar, and he watched her, smiling, as he sipped his coffee. 'Mornings,' he added, 'are Nature's way of telling us everything is going to be all right, don't you agree?' He gestured towards the window, already pink and gold with the rising sun. 'How could anything go wrong on a day that begins like this?'

'You're right,' she agreed softly, cradling the warm cup in her hands and watching with him for a moment the ecstatic miracle of dawn. Then she glanced at him. 'So,' she said. 'Do they ever talk back?'

'Who?'

'The animals.'

He assumed a very sober air. 'Oh, yes. That little fellow on the sill and I were having a very interesting discussion, as a matter of fact. All about the things that keep us places we don't want to be.'

'Like,' she suggested, 'a talented young singer with a tight schedule?'

'Among other things,' he replied, and the expression

in his eyes was filled with meaning she did not care to explore at that moment. But for some reason it made her heart beat faster.

'Oh well,' she said brightly, 'only a few more days before he arrives, and you can keep your promise to Van and be off to sunny California. What's so fascinating about that place, anyway?'

'Oh,' he replied with a lazy grin, 'lots of things. Bikinis, hot tubs, girls in pretty summer dresses . . .'

'The very necessities of life,' Lauren agreed with assumed sobriety.

He laughed. 'Did I ever tell you you're a lot of fun in the mornings, too? That's something else we have in common.'

She would have very much liked to pursue that line of conversation, and to discover what else he thought they had in common, but her new caution prevented her. She said only brightly, 'Well, I'll leave you to your conversations with animals and your dreams of hot tubs and bikinis. See you at breakfast.'

She thought a protest was forming as she turned, but she hurried away before he could say anything.

Upstairs, she set her coffee on the night-table and changed quickly into her leotard and tights. Physical activity was the only way she knew for certain to keep Shane from haunting her private thoughts, and even then he sometimes intruded. She had never really realised how much of her life he had filled when he was only, to her, a nebulous musician and poet; how much of her attitudes and emotions had been shaped by him. Now that he was a real person, multi-faceted and three-dimensional, it was inevitable that her fascination for him should be increased.

She was beginning a series of stretching exercises. In a standing position, her leg rested flat against the wall above her head while her hands gripped her ankle and her torso bent to meet it. A voice said softly behind her, 'Good lord! What are you doing?'

Pretending a casualness she did not feel, she turned

on her heel and stretched her leg out behind her, responding, 'Do you have some sort of religious objection to knocking before you enter a room?'

'I knocked,' Shane defended vaguely, watching her, 'or at least I tried. The door was open.'

Lauren was very aware of the revealing nature of the flesh-coloured leotard, which was strange, because she had spent half her life in such garments and had never before been selfconscious about it. Perhaps it had something to do with the way he was watching her as she deliberately finished the set, or perhaps it was simply his presence in her bedroom, looking so casual and rumpled, still holding the steaming mug of coffee and looking as though he belonged.

He sat on the edge of the bed, one arm hooked casually about the bedpost, sipping his coffee. 'I wish I could have seen you dance,' he said.

She was surprised, and flattered, and she hid it by sitting on the floor to begin another set of stretching exercises. She stretched one leg to the side, bent to touch her toes, straightened, and bent again. 'I wasn't all that good,' she said in a moment. 'I mean, I was good—but not destined for greatness, or anything. I suppose I always knew it,' she admitted to herself at last what Van had put into words on his first visit to the hospital. 'A dancer has a very limited on-stage life, and if success meant a starring role in a Broadway musical, then I wasn't meant for success. Of course,' she added thoughtfully, switching to the other leg, 'that really wasn't the most important thing to me. Just dancing was enough. But you wouldn't know about the struggle for success,' she said, glancing at him. 'It came easily to you.'

Shane laughed in brief astonishment. 'Success came easily to me? I spent half my life trying to live up to my father's expectations and the other half trying to escape from his shadow, and I never did learn how to do either. I still don't know what success is.'

She stopped, drawing her legs in and turning to him

as she reached for the towel she had hung on the bedpost. He handed it to her. 'I never thought about it that way,' she admitted carefully, patting her slightly damp face and neck with the towel. 'I suppose success means different things to different people.'

'In that way,' he agreed, 'you are the one who was successful. You did what you wanted to do as well as you could, for no other reason than that it gave you satisfaction. While I,' he admitted reflectively, 'even though I was doing what I wanted to do—spent too much time playing that part of the prodigal son to give anything my best effort on a consistent level. I think one of the main reasons I got into music in the first place was a misplaced sense of rebellion, but I wasn't a very good rebel after all—so, I never felt successful.'

She looked at him curiously, absently rubbing a tired back. 'Do you still feel that way about your father? Competitive and rebellious?'

Shane smiled a little. 'No, I grew out of it, along with a few other bad habits.'

'Maybe,' she suggested, 'it would be easier to find success now.'

'Maybe,' he agreed without much interest, and set his empty cup on the dresser near her bed. She was still absently massaging the small of her back, and she felt his hands slip beneath hers to take over the service. For a moment she let herself relax beneath strong, sure ministrations of his fingers which circled her back, relaxed knotted muscles, kneaded and caressed . . . but then his touch became more intimate, circling her waist, sliding up her ribs. She stood abruptly and crossed the room to pull on a wrap skirt.

He resumed his seat on the bed, watching her. 'Still mad at me, hmm?'

Lauren turned in genuine astonishment, the folds of her skirt fluttering about her calves as she tied it at the waist. 'Mad at you?' she echoed. 'Why should I be mad?'

But he only replied, watching her thoughtfully, 'I

don't really think so. We've had enough fights by now that you should be used to them, and you never did strike me as the type of person who would hold a grudge.'

'Well,' she admitted, lowering her eyes to concentrate on tying a perfect bow at her waist, 'I may not hold a grudge, but I don't think I'll ever get used to fighting with you.'

'You always had me pictured as such a meek, gentle fellow,' he supplied.

She looked at him, startled, but agreed, 'Yes.'

A momentary irritation flickered across his eyes, but he dismissed it. 'Well, fighting is good for a relationship,' he said. 'It's a great way to relieve frustration and tension, especially,' he added meaningfully, 'when there is no other outlet.'

She turned away quickly, suddenly nervous, and went over to the mirror, beginning to unwind her hair from the tight bun into which she had pinned it for exercise. But she could not escape him that easily. She could see him in the mirror, his eyes steady and thoughtful as he watched her, his position casual yet determined. 'Well,' he demanded mildly, 'what is it, then? We've about covered all the bases, you know. You've already told me you're not carrying a torch for an old lover . . .'

Now there was a question in his eyes, and she confirmed quickly, remembering his innocent enquiry about Joel when she had first arrived, 'No, of course not!' And then heat fanned her cheeks at the approval in his eyes, and she knew perfectly well where the conversation was leading.

'And you're not angry with me over anything,' he went on, rising and coming slowly over to her. 'I think I've managed to convince you that I'm not really the beast I act sometimes . . .' Again a hint of a very real question, and she nodded mutely, her eyes fastened upon his in the mirror, fumbling with hairpins and trying to look nonchalant and industrious.

Then he took her shoulders and turned her gently to

face him. The hairpins slipped from her heavy fingers and her hair spilled like honey over her shoulders. At his touch and the deep sincerity in his eyes she went weak; a pulse began to close up her throat. 'I know you've had a trauma,' he said quietly. 'I've tried to give you time to deal with it, to work out your own problems in your own way—or to help, sometimes, if I could.' Lauren swallowed hard against the sudden tightness in her throat and the softening emotions in her chest, because she knew it was true, and it was a gesture of tenderness—of caring. 'But now,' he went on, 'I think it's time we took a serious look at our relationship.'

What was he saying? A low-key panic stirred in her. Relationship? They had none, it was impossible to have one . . . And he was standing much too close, making her much too aware of him. It was against the emotions which assailed her when she was in his arms that she had to guard herself most carefully, because when she was being held by him, helpless victim to his sensuous spell, she could forget for a moment who he was, and who she was, and imagine that all sorts of things were possible.

But his eyes, so deep they were almost green and lit with a gentle light of sincerity, held her mesmerised, and she could not step away. He said, 'Lauren, you don't think I'm the type of man who would use you and leave you, do you?'

Her heart was pounding in her ears, and she could barely hear her own whispered, 'No.' No, Shane would never do anything like that. His love would be deep, it would be caring, it would be honest. He would never deliberately hurt anyone. But why was he approaching her? What was he trying to say?

A measure of relief crossed his face as he lifted one hand to lightly smooth her hair. 'Then,' he enquired gently, 'will you please tell me what's going on? You know I want to make love to you, and I think you want it too. But every time I get close to you—emotionally or physically—you draw away. Why?'

This had gone too far. In a moment he would have her believing he truly cared for her, that it was possible for something to exist between them. Lauren had to force herself to remember that he was a magician with words and she was only too vulnerable to them, for more than anything she wanted to make the fantasy come true ... She turned away, releasing herself from his spell by separating herself from his touch, and said brightly, 'Do you have to analyse everything?'

There was a pause, and she could sense him making a reluctant adjustment to the change of mood. Then he responded dryly, 'That's something else we have in common.' He perched casually on the edge of the dressing-table, and went on. 'I'm not leaving until I get an answer, you know. What is it about me that makes you think twice every time I come near you? Are you afraid of me—of men in general?'

'Don't be silly!' No, she wasn't afraid of him, or of making love ... not when that was what she wanted above all things in the world. But her hand fumbled with the thin gold chain at her neck in a nervous gesture, and she refused to turn to look at him.

'All right.' There was a note in his voice, beneath the assumed calmness, which suggested he was fighting impatience. 'Then it must be that you're afraid I'm just playing games with you ...' There was a wry twist to his tone as he added, 'That I see you as an easy conquest and I won't respect you in the morning and all of that other lovely nonsense, right?'

'Maybe,' she retorted lightly, stepping towards the window to draw back the curtains, 'I'm just afraid of disappointing you.' And she did not realise how close that was to the truth until she had said it.

Shane's short, incredulous laugh behind her was sharp with sarcasm and amazement. '*You*'re afraid of disappointing *me*? Wow, that's rich!' She heard him stand and begin to cross the room towards her, and her cheeks burned. She had never meant to reveal so much of herself to him, and she had done it so clumsily and

unwittingly. 'How would you like,' he demanded
behind her, 'to try to live up to the image someone has
built of you as a combination Albert Einstein and
Prince Charles?'

She whirled, cheeks flaming and eyes snapping. 'I
never——'

'Lauren, don't you think I can tell it? he
expostulated, and anger was becoming intermixed with
incredulity. 'It's in your eyes every time you look at
me—I hung the stars in place, it personally supervised
the placement of every blade of grass and painted the
rainbow, and as far as you're concerned, Johann
Sebastian Bach could have taken lessons from me! For
heaven's sake, Lauren, do you have any idea how
hard that is to deal with?'

She retreated a few steps, shaking her head,
miserable with embarrassment and anger. Shane
reached for her arm, but she jerked away, and
managed, 'I think you're overestimating yourself! I
never——'

'I only wish I were!' This time he caught her arm,
fastening his fingers about her wrist. Amazement,
desperation, and disappointment were streaked across
his face. 'That's really it, isn't it?' he demanded. 'You
are really afraid of disappointing me—you think you're
not good enough for me!' And even though she shook
her head mutely, there was no way to convincingly deny
what he had so accurately pinpointed. And he saw it in
her eyes, because there was sudden hurt there, and the
pressure of his fingers increased about her wrist. 'For
Pete's sake, Lauren, I'm human!' He jerked her hand
forward and placed it roughly against his face, his
throat, his chest. 'Touch me—feel me! I'm just a man
who wants you, and . . .'

He broke off as he looked at her, her eyes wide
with the onslaught of his temper and her own
embarrassment. Slowly he released a breath, his
eyelids dropped, and his fingers entwined with hers
against his chest. He reached his arm about her waist

and drew her gently to him, simply holding her in mute apology.

And that gesture was all it took. The embarrassment and the indignation faded away into his tenderness, understanding flowed from her as it did from him. Her free arm crept about his neck and she was drowning in the warm emotions his embrace communicated. This moment was what she had waited for all her life; why had she been so afraid to accept it?

'You may not believe this,' he said after a moment, 'but I do have trouble putting certain emotions into words.'

'Don't tell me what I believe,' she murmured against his shoulder, her heart quickening in anticipation.

His arm tightened about her briefly, then he stepped back, looking down at her soberly. 'Lauren, I care about you,' he said simply. 'It hurts me to think that I'm the cause of your feeling bad about yourself—that I in any way cause you to feel like less of a woman, or less than a person. Can you understand that?'

She nodded, lowering her eyes to their clasped hands. 'I'm sorry,' she managed in a moment, and it was difficult. 'It's just that I've known you so much longer than you've known me, and I had so many preconceived ideas about you, and I—I did worship you, I guess.' She ventured a shy glance at him. 'And I couldn't—can't imagine that you would ... why you would ...' And she floundered, unable to finish.

Shane tipped her chin upwards with his finger. 'You can't understand why I would be interested in you,' he said quietly. His eyes were very steady, deeply perceptive. 'How can I explain that? You're lovely and sensitive, and when I'm with you I sometimes feel a sort of harmony that I never have with anyone else. You make me want to share with you, you make me understand things about myself I never did before. I look at you,' he added softly, 'and I see in you things about yourself you don't see, and that makes me feel special.'

'You are special,' she whispered, her eyes searching his, inviting his, drawing him closer.

And then he dropped his eyes. A muscle near his cheek tightened, and he slowly unwound his fingers from hers. 'But the harmony never lasts,' he said briefly, 'because of this barrier between us. I can't really share myself with you because sooner or later I'm bound to hurt you, when you discover I don't live up to your expectations ... You give me a glimpse of promises that can never be. And I don't think I can live with that.'

A cold stream slowly replaced the warm liquid which had been pulsing through her veins; the tingling thrill she had felt in his arms turned into a shiver as he stepped away. She lost her breath and her speech in the sinking disappointment that congealed in her stomach, and she could only watch Shane cross the room in dull confusion. The moment was gone, as it so often was between them, as abruptly as it had come, and she did not know how to recapture it ... and the worst of the aching despair was in suspecting it would never come again.

Then he turned, the expression on his face relaxed, polite, and casual—as though none of what had gone before had ever taken place. 'I almost forgot,' he said pleasantly, 'why I came up here in the first place.'

With a great effort, Lauren assumed some of his negligent air. 'Oh? Why?'

'Van and Marie are having another one of their parties this weekend, and I thought you might like to get away from the social whirl for a few hours. I have tickets to a show in Denver; we can have dinner at a quiet little restaurant and take in some culture for a change.'

She managed, just barely, a laugh. 'That sounds like exchanging one social whirl for another. What's the show?'

He watched her carefully. '*A Chorus Line.*'

She dropped her eyes, waiting for the hurt to come. *A*

Chorus Line, that smash Broadway musical that depicted the lives of the unsung heroes of the theatre—her life. It was the dream of every dancer to appear in that show, he surely must know what even the mention of the title would mean to her. And she waited for the pain, the anger, the frustrated raging at fate to begin inside her—but, curiously, it never did. Still, she responded cautiously, looking at him, 'I've seen it.'

'So have I.' His voice was even, his eyes very steady. 'I thought it was about time we saw it together.'

She caught the inside of her inner lip between her teeth, wondering once again what meaning lay behind the words he would not reveal. Only caring, she realised slowly. Shane was only showing that he cared for her, and still wanted to share with her ... She did not hesitate much longer. 'Thanks,' she said steadily, her eyes quietly accepting the gesture and the reason for it. 'I'd like that.'

He smiled, and even though it was only a quiet, tender smile, it seemed the whole room was suddenly bathed in brilliance. 'Good,' he said simply, and closed the door behind him.

The next two days were rainy and cold, and their morning walks were eliminated. Shane was busy with long-distance phone calls to his own studio or in consultation with Van, and Lauren was busy helping Marie prepare for the Saturday night party. But even though they saw very little of one another, the warm glow with which he had left her on their last meeting remained and regenerated. Something was changing, and she was not certain whether it was within her or between them. In his presence she was relaxed and content, and when she was away from him he filled her thoughts. She awoke happy and full of energy, and at night he hovered over her dreams like a benediction—a warm, subtle presence which could not be analysed, but which filled her with tranquillity simply because it was there. She had never felt more alive in her life.

By Saturday the rain had cleared, but the temperature was dropping and the sky remained heavy with lead-coloured clouds. At breakfast Van commented, 'Looks like the beginning of winter is at hand.' And Marie worried about the possibility of severe weather which might ruin the party.

Lauren glanced at Shane, afraid the brewing storm might cancel their own plans, but his smile was reassuring. She settled back to finish her meal happily.

Marie and Van were not the least bit insulted that their two house guests preferred not to attend their party. As a matter of fact, since Lauren and Shane were leaving early to allow plenty of time for dinner before the show, Marie was able to devote her full attention to helping Lauren dress, and she did it with enthusiasm.

Lauren chose, from the few party dresses she had brought with her, a wine-coloured velvet, simple yet regal. It was gathered at the waist into a modified bell skirt which fell just above the calves. The sleeves were dropped below the shoulder and their full cut gathered at the wrist with a tiny ruching of white cotton lace which was repeated at the high neckline. Marie took from her own jewellery collection a mid-length strand of pearls which shone richly against the velvet background. Lauren, who as a rule wore very little jewellery, was awed by the effect, and she fingered the strand nervously.

'I'll be so afraid I might lose them,' she protested, 'I won't be able to think about anything else.'

'Oh, yes, you will,' Marie assured her with a maternal smile, presenting the matching earrings. 'You'll be thinking about how beautiful you look and how all the other women are trying to keep their husbands' eyes off you ... and about what a wonderful time you're having.'

Marie brushed Lauren's hair into a stylish knot at the side of her head and, as a finishing touch, added a silver comb which was threaded with velvet ribbon the colour of her dress. The ribbons dangled attractively just below her left ear, and Lauren was thrilled with the effect. They both stepped back to observe the result of the efforts in the mirror, and Marie practically beamed as she hugged her shoulders. 'Perfect,' she announced. 'You look—radiant, and,' she added slyly, 'I'm not at all sure that has anything to do with the colour of your dress.'

Lauren laughed and noticed that the rich velvet did seem to be reflected in her face, making her eyes shine as softly as the pearls at her throat. But she also knew the colour had little to do with costuming ... it was happiness, pure and simple. She was going out with Shane, for the first time they would have an evening entirely to themselves, and she could not have been more excited if it had been her first date.

Shane was in the living room, talking with Van, when she came down. He was dressed in a dark suit and pale grey striped tie, and his hair was fluffy and shiny against the white collar. Gold cufflinks gleamed at his wrists and he looked every inch the gentleman, comfortable and at ease in the fine attire.

He turned when she walked in, and his eyes reflected the sincerity of his words. 'You look,' he said softly, and paused for just a moment in his selection of just the right adjective, 'elegant.'

The compliment was all the more dear because of the thoughtfulness and sincerity which had backed it, and was so typical of him. He could have said 'beautiful' or 'marvellous', but those were stock phrases, often meaningless. He had searched for the exact word to pinpoint his meaning and to reflect the way she felt, and a thrill of happiness rushed through her as she came over to him.

'I've never seen you in a dress before,' he added, a sparkle in his eye as he swept her up and down. 'There should be a law that woman can wear nothing else.'

'I've never seen you in anything other than jeans, either,' she retorted lightly, teasing him. 'The transformation is incredible!'

He laughed and took her arm, and Marie and Van watched like benevolent parents as they left the house.

The hour drive to Denver was peaceful and pleasant, marred only once by Shane's comment, 'I have to get back to L.A. pretty soon. Work is piling up on me, and there's only so much I can do over the telephone.'

Lauren glanced at him, trying to subdue the crushing disappointment which seemed out of place on this, what promised to be the most perfect night of her life. The look she met in his eyes told her he was gently trying to prepare her for his leaving, and, in truth, she should have been prepared for it long ago. She turned her eyes back to the dusty mountain road and asked, as casually as she could, 'When will you leave?'

'A couple of weeks at the outside.' Still, she felt his eyes on her as he divided his attention between the road and the expression on her face.

The next question was more difficult. 'Will—you come back?'

Her eyes were wide and grey as they looked at him in the twilight, and they met a gentle smile. 'Probably,' he said, and reached for her hand.

She wrapped her fingers about his and contented herself with that, which, when he said it, sounded more like a promise than an uncertainty.

The restaurant he had chosen was suited to her mood: romantic, beautifully appointed, elegant. Damask tableclothes, heavy silver, and a vase of budding roses complemented every table. Their table overlooked the twinkling lights of the city below and the shadowy mountains in the background, and Lauren's eyes sparkled with the pleasure of it all as she breathed a soft, luxurious sigh of contentment.

'I've often imagined you in a setting like this,' Shane smiled. 'Why haven't we done it before?'

'Because you never asked me?' suggested Lauren lightly, and his eyes twinkled in response.

'Then I promise to correct that in the future,' he assured her, and lifted his glass to her in salute.

As the salad course was served, Shane enquired, 'Did Van mention to you the big concert he's getting together for the spring?'

Lauren shook her head, interested.

'Well, I shouldn't say "he", specifically, but several of the top studios are throwing in with some concert promoters to introduce their spring releases in a giant concert in Dodger Stadium. It promises to be pretty exciting—a day-long pop festival, sort of like a modified Woodstock.'

'Greatly modified, I hope,' she put in, and he grinned. She took a bite of her salad, which was rich with creamy blue cheese and spicy bits of watercress, and then queried, 'Will you be there?'

'I doubt it,' he answered, turning to his own salad. 'Van enjoys racing all over the world keeping his hand in this sort of thing, but I stick strictly to producing records. Besides, I imagine I'll have my hands full this winter as it is, searching out sentimental love songs to fill the albums we've already contracted for.'

Lauren hesitated a moment, then commented, 'You never did any love songs.'

He looked confused. 'What?'

'That was one thing I always noticed about you,' she explained. 'You didn't sing love songs. I mean, sometimes you sang *about* it, but it was always in the third person, and almost in passing. I just thought it was curious.'

Shane seemed to puzzle at that for a moment. 'You know,' he admitted at last, 'I guess you're right, I never really thought about it before.'

'Any reason?' she pursued innocently.

'Maybe,' he answered thoughtfully, and she could tell as he looked at her he was being perfectly honest, 'because I didn't know anything about love.'

She felt a pang for him as she thought about his lonely childhood in an impersonal family, his unhappy marriage which had ended in tragedy, the bleak sense of isolation which had communicated itself in so many of his songs. She remembered the warmth of her own family, the happiness which had surrounded her growing up years and the support which had continued throughout her young adulthood . . . and even when her own parents were gone there had been Marie and Van to step in, every bit as concerned and supportive as natural parents would have been. Lauren's life had not been without its hardships, but there had always been love. I have so much to give you, she thought, and as she smiled at him across the candlelit table there was a moment of quiet ecstasy because she realised for the first time that it was true. She *did* have something to offer him, if only he would accept it . . .

The beef bourguignon was superb, and for a time Lauren let the conversation lag as she devoted herself to the full enjoyment of her meal. Shane watched her indulgently, and commented, 'I'm glad to see your appetite has improved.'

She laughed a little, touching her napkin to her lips and taking a sip of wine. 'I suppose I was a pretty sorry sight when I first came here,' she answered.

'Understandable.' He took up his own glass. 'After the accident,' he went on, unexpectedly, 'I went through something of the same thing. Shock, depression . . .' His voice grew heavy with the pain of those memories, and though his eyes were veiled with sadness the usual impenetrable barrier was not there. He wanted to talk about it, to share it with her, and something within her quickened in response to him. 'I had a really hard time adjusting. I sometimes think—no, I know—that I haven't completely. I started to build a new life for myself, and it's not one that I dislike, but it's as though . . .' again he paused in search or just the right words, 'as though I'm constantly living in that misty, musky time just before dawn, waiting for the sun to break through.' His smile was vague, and tender. 'But you— you don't spend your time wandering through the twilight. You gave your grief its proper course, just as you should have, and then you got over it. You made up your mind to recover, and that's exactly what you're doing. I admire that,' he told her honestly. 'I wish I had the power to make my life that simple.'

Her hands were folded in her lap, her eyes softened with empathy and gratitude. I love you, she thought slowly, but surely. I love you for sharing this with me, for making me a part of your life at last. I love you just as I always have done, but more, and differently . . . and better. For slowly, inexorably, Shane was becoming a real person to her, opening himself for her to discover, and she was finding only what had been there all along, but she had been too blind to see.

Perhaps he noticed a changing expression in her eyes, or perhaps he simply sensed the intensifying of the atmosphere around them and was unprepared to maintain the mood. The smile he gave her then was light, and he turned back to his meal, guiding the conversation on to more neutral subjects.

I love you, she thought in utter serenity. It's that simple.

The show was a blur of bright colours, glittering costumes, stunning choreography and haunting music, but the sparkle paled before the dazzling emotions which danced inside her. Shane held her hand, and when once or twice she leaned over to whisper a comment to him his answering smile filled her with quiet joy. For two hours they shared a world which had once been hers but was no longer, and the fact that they shared it replaced any lingering sense of loss with a discovery so precious it filled every corner of her with the promise of things to come. She was not alone, and at that moment she did not think she would ever be again. Shane was there for her . . . just as he had always been.

When they came out the streets were blanketed with another unexpected pleasure—a deep, silent drift of snow. Lauren gave an exclamation of delight and lifted her hands to catch the fast-falling flakes of snow, feeling it powder her hair and splash against her face.

'Perfect!' she cried. 'What a lovely way to end the evening!'

Shane gave her a wry look. 'I hope you'll still say so when I tell you we're not driving home in this.'

She stared at him. 'What? But what will we do? What do you mean?'

He took her arm to lead her towards the car. 'I mean it's too dangerous,' he said briefly. 'We'll wait until morning when the snow-ploughs have been through.'

Her astonishment slowed her steps. 'What do you mean—morning? Shane, that's ridiculous! What will we do, where will we stay? You can't be serious! Just because of a little snow——'

'It will be more than a little snow towards the mountains,' he returned shortly, and she could feel tension in the muscles of his arm beneath her fingers. 'We'll stay in town until the road conditions improve in the morning. No argument,' he finished firmly as she opened her mouth once again to protest.

Her confusion was only increased when, at the hotel, he registered them in separate rooms. Until that point she might have thought it was some sort of elaborate joke, or even—though it did not seem Shane's style—a not-so-subtle way of suggesting to her that the evening would be more appropriately ended by something other than returning to their separate bedrooms under Marie's and Van's supervision. But he was very businesslike as he secured their keys and presented one to her, and he spoke little in the elevator.

'I don't have anything to wear,' she complained as they made their way down the carpeted hall. 'This is a ridiculous expense, you know. I'm sure the roads aren't that bad . . . I don't even have a toothbrush!'

He found her room number and opened the door, returning her key to her. 'I'm right next door,' he said blandly, 'if you need me.'

And she watched in incredulous astonishment as he turned and entered his own room.

She closed her door and sat heavily on the edge of the

bouncy bed, rigid with discontent and confusion. What a man of mysteriously changing moods he was! Not even a goodnight . . . And after the wonderful closeness they had shared all evening. She kicked off her shoes and lay back on the bed, staring at the ceiling, weary with too many emotions at once, thinking back over the events of the evening, treasuring the time he had shared with her.

And then it occurred to her slowly, something so simple she should have surely realised it before, and impatience filled her at her own insensitivity. For Shane was still sharing with her, and expecting her to understand . . . Unpleasant memories and a dread of snow, a fatal accident perhaps caused by a slippery road, a caution which was not so unreasonable after all . . . Again, she softened in empathy with him, and peace filled her as she once again felt in harmony with him.

After a time she got up and washed the make-up off her face, took down her hair, and removed her pantyhose and her dress. It would not be the first time she had slept in her slip, or without the amenities of a few basic toiletries, and she remembered lost luggage and mixed-up reservations with a wry grimace as she prepared to get into bed.

A knock on the communicating door startled her, and Shane's voice called, 'It's just me. Unless you're shockingly indecent, I'm coming in.'

She found an extra blanket on the luggage rack and was wrapping herself in it just as he came through the door.

'Charming,' he commented on the clumsily wrapped blanket, and there was a spark of amusement in his eye. 'Toothbrush,' he announced, and handed it to her, 'and toothpaste. Just so you don't feel completely cut off from civilisation.'

Lauren slipped her arm out to retrieve the items while trying to maintain a hold on the blanket. 'Thanks,' she said, smiling uncertainly at him. 'You didn't have to . . .'

He shrugged it off. 'It was the least I could do. I called Marie and told her we were all right, and to expect us in the morning. She said,' he added pointedly, 'that a lot of their guests are staying overnight because the roads are so bad.'

She dropped her eyes in contrition and turned to place the toothbrush kit on the dresser. But she turned again when he spoke.

'Lauren,' he said quietly, 'I want you to know I didn't plan this. I have a—thing about driving in bad weather, and I didn't want to take any chances with you in the car.' His smile was slightly uneasy, as though wondering whether she would accept that. 'Another one of my faults.'

'I understand,' she told him simply, and the lines on his face smoothed out into more natural, relaxed ones.

'In that case, then . . .' He came forward and took her shoulders. 'May I kiss you goodnight?'

She laughed, tipping her face upwards to him. 'You couldn't before?'

'Not as long as you were still thinking this was some sort of elaborate seduction scheme,' he responded, and the deep light she loved so well was in his eyes as he softly touched her hair. 'It was a good evening, wasn't it, Lauren?'

She whispered, 'Yes.' And his lips touched hers.

It was meant to be a goodnight kiss, simple, tender, brief. She knew that. But she didn't know how to control her response, which was natural and right and completely overwhelming, for in that moment everything she loved about Shane seemed to bubble up and demand release. Her arms crept about his neck and the blanket fell away unheeded. She felt his cautious intake of breath, the surprise and question, and then his hands were upon her waist, against the thin, silky material of her slip, caressing and delighting in the feel of it even as she delighted in the sensation of his strong fingers against her skin with nothing more than the fine layer of material separating them. His hand slipped about to cup her breast, fingers gently exploring, coaxing her to a new and heightened state of arousal, and her knees went weak with the tingling sensations of passion that swept through her.

She was sitting on the bed, then lying back upon it, his breath was hot against her cheek, and her ear, and her neck, and the evidence of his restraint was in the slow, gently caressing course his hand traced along her leg, beneath her slip, feathering against the inside of her thigh and further upward to her bare abdomen. The moment was upon them, and it seemed as though it had been carved from destiny. It was right and it was good, she had waited for it all her life, and she gave herself over to it joyously.

Shane had removed his coat and tie before coming in, and the shirt was unbuttoned already at the collar. It was an easy task, and it seemed the most natural thing in the world, for Lauren to release the remaining buttons, baring his chest for the embrace of her arms, her fingers exploring the smooth skin of his back, experiencing the tautness of his shoulders and the length of his muscles. Her hands swept lightly across his chest, delighting in the sensation of soft chest hair which tingled in her fingertips like static electricity. She felt the surprising quiver of his flesh as her fingers brushed across his breast and his soft, indrawn breath, and he cupped her face in his hands as his lips found her again, giving her a kiss that was powerful with desire but gentle in its restraint. Her hands explored the smooth, firm muscles of his abdomen, and the catch of his trousers, and slowly his lips left hers.

'Lauren,' he whispered, and she opened her eyes. Everything was blurred with the heat of passion and the warmth of his body next to hers, and she could not read the expression in his eyes. He took her fingers and brought them to his lips, and that simple, lingering kiss brought a new dimension to passion, to caring. His voice was slightly breathless and had a husky timbre, and she noticed that his eyes were so dark they seemed to have no colour at all as he said softly, 'Who is it you're going to make love with—Shane Holt the musician, or simply myself, the man?'

It seemed a strange question, confusing and irrelevant. But it seemed important to him that she answer, and there was no doubt in her mind what the answer would be. She loved him, all of him, didn't he know that by now? She whispered, tightening her fingers about his, 'They're one and the same, Shane.'

Slowly he released her hand. He turned away, he stood. She thought he would finish undressing, or simply turn off the light; she was completely unprepared for the steps he took towards the door.

'I'm sorry Lauren,' he said quietly. 'That's just not good enough.'

She pushed herself upwards, every muscle in her body suddenly trembling and cold, and weakness drained into horror as she realised he was leaving. She hardly had enough breath to whisper, and it came out in a choked, croaking sound. 'Shane, what did I do? Why . . .'

'I won't be part of your fantasy,' he returned briefly. 'Not any more.'

But it wasn't a fantasy! Couldn't he see that? He was only the man she loved forever, first in dreams and now in reality, and she only wanted to share that love . . . But she could not speak.

With his hand on the doorknob, he turned to look at her, and the stark pain and disappointment in his eyes sent a pain through her chest; she hugged herself against a violent shiver and she wanted to reach out to him and comfort him, but she was helpless against what she saw in his face. 'I wanted to be loved by you,' he said, very low, 'more than anything else in the world. But not this way. Not . . .' he opened the door, and the last words were hardly above a whisper, 'this way.'

The door closed softly behind him, and Lauren was alone.

CHAPTER EIGHT

'I WANTED to be loved by you . . .' The words haunted an endless night as tears streamed silently down her temples and soaked the cold pillow beneath her head. And she wanted only to love him, to comfort his troubled spirit and make him happy. But she could not reach him. What she had to give was not what he wanted after all. She had had the love of a lifetime within fingertips' grasp and had somehow let it slip away . . . and there was nothing she could do about it. Nothing at all.

She dragged herself out of bed at dawn, washed her face, and was dressed by the time Shane knocked softly on the communicating door. She had a pounding headache from sleeplessness and worry, and she found it difficult to return his rather strained smile. He, too, looked pale and worn, but there was no satisfaction in knowing he had slept no better than she had.

They spoke hardly at all on the way downstairs. Shane offered her breakfast, and Lauren refused. He looked as though he understood.

The day was clear and brilliant, but crystal cold. The snow-plough had been through and ribbons of asphalt gleamed between blinding white banks as they made their way out of the city. The car was warm, but Lauren was cold. The near-silent purr of the motor was rhythmic and soothing, but it only pulsed new waves of pain through her head. The silence between them was unbearable. They had to talk about it. Would they never talk about it? Would Shane try to ignore it, to pretend nothing of consequence had happened, and one day just walk away not knowing, or caring, that her entire life had been changed within the space of a few seconds last night in his presence?

At last she requested, trying to keep the tension out of her voice. 'Could we have the radio on, please?'

He turned it on, and Shane Holt's voice from an old recording floated through the speakers:

> The sun is on the mountain
> and it hovers like a prize
> for all the things left yet untouchable,
> But there's winter in your eyes,
> And I must go . . .

Oh, no, thought Lauren in aching despair. Even now he has just the right words . . . and he switched it off.

He said unexpectedly, 'Don't hate me.'

She looked at him, a quick breath and a startled protest on her lips, but his face was hard and expressionless, his eyes fastened upon the road. He said evenly, 'I don't expect you to understand, just listen. I know I acted badly last night and I'm sorry. The last thing in the world I want is to hurt you . . . but I don't want to be hurt, either.' She saw his hands tighten on the steering wheel, and the muscle near his jaw was prominent. She wanted to see his eyes, but he would not allow it. 'I can't help hurting you, Lauren, don't you see that? I can't help disappointing you, because what you're expecting of me is something I can't give.'

'That's not true,' she said quietly. 'It may have been once, but . . . not any more.'

He glanced at her, and she could tell he wanted to believe her, but he did not. 'You look at me,' he said, 'and you see the man who never existed. But it's worse . . . you try to make him come alive, and you drag up a past that's——' He struggled over the words. 'Not pleasant for me to see. I get angry when you take me back to a time I've tried so hard to forget, and when I see the difference between what you think I am and what I really am, it makes me—ashamed. I can't deal with it.'

She turned to him earnestly, her arm resting along

the back of the car seat, yearning to touch him but not daring. 'I only want to care for you,' she said softly. 'You said you wanted it too.'

'I expected too much,' he replied shortly. His knuckles on the steering wheel were white.

'Why won't you help me understand?' she pleaded. 'You're closing doors to me, you won't let me get close. You can't just tell me what I'm doing wrong, you have to *show* me. Why does the past frighten you so much? You have nothing to be ashamed of! Oh, Shane, don't you know that I lo——'

'I don't want to talk any more,' he cut her off coldly, and she shrank back as though struck. When he glanced at her there was a flicker of softening in his eyes, a hint of regret, and his voice lost its curtness as he turned back to the road. 'I'm very tired,' he said simply, heavily.

And that, apparently, was the way he wanted to leave it.

The next few days Shane was remote, polite yet distant, very quiet . . . and not just to Lauren, but to everyone in the house. There was a vagueness in his eyes, as though he were fighting a deeply troubling battle within himself and could accept no aid. Too many times Lauren discovered him standing at the window, looking out at the snow, and there was a thinly disguised impatience there, a restlessness which would not be stilled. She knew she was losing him, and the knowledge curled into a dull, aching pain deep within the core of her which left her neither day or night.

And then Jimmy Wild arrived, and changed all their lives.

Lauren did not know what she had expected. A long-haired, hyper-energetic, freewheeling rock musician, perhaps, like the members of Angel's band. Or a moody, ultra-sensitive, prima donna type—certainly not the earnest young man who turned out to be Jimmy Wild.

He arrived on a blustery winter day, plainly dressed in a brown suit which looked as though it had seen better days, his neatly combed brown hair frosted with snow, looking nervous, awed, and cold. He was easily impressed and overly appreciative, as though slightly dazzled by the trip and the house and all that had happened to him—a trait which Lauren and Marie found charming, and Van found amusing. But when Jimmy made the mistake of calling Shane 'Sir' Lauren did not know whether to burst into giggles or hold her breath for the young man's sake, remembering how Shane had reacted to her gesture of respect on their first meeting and knowing that he was in no mood to be kind to strangers. His sharp tongue could carve the young man to shreds in less than a sentence and completely destroy whatever confidence he had left, and Lauren did not think she could ever forgive him for that. But to her relief, and much to Shane's credit, he simply replied that no one had called him 'sir' since R.O.T.C. training in high school and that, as he had a terrible memory for names, it would probably be much better all around if everyone remained on a first-name basis while they were working together. There was a gentling of his features while he spoke to Jimmy, one that Lauren had not seen in too long, and she loved him for that.

From that point, Jimmy seemed to relax slowly, and as Marie served spiced wine and hot hors d'oeuvres in the living room he talked about himself and his music. Often while he was speaking his eyes would flicker to Lauren as though seeking reassurance, possibly because she was the closest to his age or the only one present who could not intimidate him with power, and she always answered with an encouraging smile. She liked him.

He was twenty-four years old and had started playing with a rock band when he was thirteen. He had never been out of his native state of Indiana, and he had been performing as a single with various back-up bands for the past five years. He liked what he was doing. It was steady employment, and stability was important to him. But, beyond that, he loved making music simply for its own sake. When he talked about music all hints of awkwardness and shyness were gone, his eyes were lit by a quiet sort of passion, and he was in his element. Although he did not say so directly, it was obvious he had no overt ambitions to be a star, but, from the look which passed from Van to Shane, Lauren knew he had the makings of one. And then Shane asked to hear him play.

Jimmy's eyes lit up with greedy delight as he saw all the equipment in the music room, but he chose a twelve-string acoustic guitar, positioned himself with natural ease before a microphone, and did not notice when Van turned on the recorder. He chose a simple ballad, and from the moment he began to sing a sort of hushed awe fell over the room, the spell in which he captured his audience of four was a tangible thing. Completely involved with himself, the love he felt for his art flowed from the strings of his instrument and from his voice and made it beautiful. Midway through the chorus Van joined him in back-up on the synthesiser, but Jimmy hardly noticed. Watching him, Lauren was struck by something achingly familiar about his performance, something heartrending yet indefinable. You are going to make it, Jimmy Wild, she thought in quiet exultation. You really are.

When he was finished, the moment of reverent silence endured. There was triumph in Van's eyes, and a mist of tears in Marie's. But it was to Shane that Jimmy looked, and to Lauren's shock, Shane, stony-faced, said abruptly, 'Excuse me,' and left the room.

For a moment they all stared after him, then Van got up and followed him. Jimmy, shielding his eyes as he carefully replaced the guitar, said softly, 'Wow! That bad, huh?'

Marie assured him quickly, 'You were fantastic!' There was impatience with Shane in her eyes even as she defended him. 'You mustn't let Shane bother you. He's temperamental, and he's been moody lately, but that won't affect his judgment of your performance. It's just that——' She looked to Lauren for help.

'You remind him of himself,' Lauren realised slowly. Jimmy's eyes flew to hers in surprise, and she explained, 'You could be Shane ten years ago. He saw it as soon as I did—it was like looking into a mirror on the past.'

Jimmy shook his head in wonder and disbelief. 'There's only one Shane Holt.'

'And there's only one Jimmy Wild,' Lauren assured him firmly. 'And I think you've just found the one man in the world who can understand your music and turn it into something special. The two of you couldn't make a more perfect team.'

There was uneasiness in Jimmy's eyes as he sat down at the synthesiser and absently fingered the silent keyboard. 'I don't know. Maybe this whole thing was a big mistake. I only agreed to it because . . .' he glanced at Marie with a slightly apologetic smile, 'you don't turn down a man like Marvin Van Fossen.'

'Oh, but surely,' protested Marie, 'you wouldn't consider turning down a contract with one of the biggest recording studios in the business. It's the chance of a lifetime!'

'Sure it is,' agreed Jimmy sensibly, 'but it could also be the biggest fall of my lifetime. A contract doesn't make you a star, and neither does one hit. I'm pretty satisfied with my life the way it is right now, and to tell you the truth, I don't know that I'm all that crazy about being a star, even if I do make it. It's all so risky.'

'Think of the money,' prompted Marie.

'I am,' Jimmy agreed glumly, and just then Shane returned.

He had a drink in his hand, and his stance was relaxed, but beneath the casual demeanor Lauren could sense a quiet turmoil. He told Jimmy briefly, 'You're good. I think we can talk a deal, but I'm going to have to hear how you come across on tape—after all, we're talking recording contracts, here. I know you brought some demos, but if you're not too tired, I'd like to make a couple of more here tonight, and then tomorrow we'll go to the studio for some good back-up sound. What do you say we get started?'

There was excitement in Jimmy's eyes as he looked at Lauren, but it was still tempered with a measure of caution. She gave him a wink and a sign of encouragement with her thumb and forefinger, and left the professionals to their work.

After breakfast two days later Jimmy's work was finished. Shane and Van locked themselves in the music room with his tapes, and had lunch served to them there. During the afternoooon Jimmy wandered about looking forlorn and worried, and Lauren felt sorry for him. The two producers made an appearance at dinner but their conversation was mostly technical, and they gave Jimmy neither a sign of encouragement or discouragement—and, in fact, hardly addressed themselves to him at all. After dinner they returned to the music room, and Jimmy hung about the kitchen as the women cleared the dishes, trying to make himself useful while his fate rested in the hands of two virtual strangers.

To distract him, Lauren challenged him to a video game, and, although he agreed readily enough, it was obvious his mind was not on the game. Lauren, who was a terrible player, completely massacred him in the first three games, and finally she demanded in exasperation, 'They were good, weren't they?'

He looked up absently. 'What?'

'Your tapes. Weren't they good?'

'Yeah.' He smiled a little. 'Yeah, they were good.'

She sat down on the sofa, making a sweeping gesture with her arm to dismiss his anxieties. 'Then you have nothing to worry about. You look like they've already set the execution date!'

He laughed a little and came to sit beside her. 'Yeah, I know. I just feel like I'm in way over my head. I mean, men like Shane Holt and Marvin Van Fossen—they're superstars in the business; I'm just a small town boy. And I'm homesick. I miss my family.'

The admission was endearing, and she smiled at him. She had known he was married, but she asked, 'Do you have children?'

'Two,' he answered, then he grinned. 'I don't suppose you'd be interested in seeing some pictures?'

She enthusiastically agreed, and curled her feet beneath her as he opened his wallet and took out a collection of photographs of two boys in various stages of development. 'This is Bear,' he pointed out a picture of a tough-looking, husky little kid in a baseball cap, scowling at the camera. 'His real name is Richard, but he'll never be anything but a Bear. Looks like one too, doesn't he?' Lauren laughingly agreed, and he went on, 'He started kindergarten this year and terrorised the whole class. For a while there I thought we might be the first parents to have their son expelled from kindergarten ... This is Mickey. He's three, and thinks his big brother told God how to create the earth. This is my wife, Jean.'

Lauren glanced at him. 'Neither one of you looked old enough to have two children.'

'Yeah, well, we married right out of high school.' He looked at the pictures fondly for a moment longer, then reluctantly put them away. 'Not because we had to either,' he went on, tucking his wallet back into his pocket. 'We were childhood sweethearts, the kind of thing everyone said wouldn't last, but somehow it did.' He was thoughtful for a moment, then he looked at her seriously. 'You know what's really bothering me?' he demanded. 'I'm not sure whether I'm afraid they won't offer me a contract, or they will. If they do, I'm not sure what I'll say.'

Lauren could not help showing her surprise, and he explained, 'I know no one is offering me instant stardom, and I'm not afraid of failing—hell, I've failed before, and I can take it. I don't mind working hard

'Well,' Shane assured him with a smile, 'I'm not making any promises. I mean, you're not going to be opening for the Stones on a world tour any time soon, but we are going to do our best to put your name on the charts within the next year. Now, can we talk about a deal?'

'Yeah,' Jimmy replied dazedly, 'sure. Of course!' And then he laughed, shaking his head a little as though to clear it of the fog. 'Listen, I'm sorry, this is just all hitting me pretty hard . . . You're going to think this is hokey, but would you mind if I called my wife first? She's been waiting all week . . .'

'Go ahead,' Shane told him, and the smile in his eyes was genuine. 'Always keep your priorities straight. And Jimmy . . .' he extended his hand to him, 'good to have you aboard.'

Jimmy laughed, shook his hand enthusiastically, and practically skipped out of the room.

Her new friend's happiness was reflected on Lauren's face as she turned to Shane. 'I'm so glad,' she said, 'that it worked out.'

'I'm sure you are.' Though his tone was mild, the hardness was back in his eyes, and that startled her. 'You two seemed very close.'

Her eyes widened with amused insult. 'And just what is that supposed to mean?'

'Just what I said.' He crossed the room and idly placed a video cartridge in the player. 'That was a cosy scene I walked in on.'

'Oh, for goodness' sake!' she exclaimed impatiently. 'He's married!'

'So?' He flipped a switch and a series of toneless, monotonous beeps floated from the machine.

'You're not accusing me of chasing after a married man?'

'I don't know you well enough to accuse you of anything,' he replied flatly, and turned the machine off.

Lauren could not take him seriously, and she refused to be hurt. 'Well,' she said easily, coming over to him, 'I must say I'm surprised. Instead of insulting me, you should be thanking me. I just saved a recording artist for you. He wasn't going to sign.'

'And you just did him the favour of his life,' returned Shane bitterly, not looking at her. 'Living out another fantasy, Lauren?'

He was really serious, and she caught her breath. 'What,' she asked cautiously, 'do you mean by that?'

There was fury in his eyes as he turned on her. 'The original wasn't good enough for you, was it? So you turn to an exact copy and hope you have better luck! And why not—it's just perfect! In fantasies little things like wives and children and pasts and character don't matter—you just want a cardboard cut-out you can fit into your dream! Well, I wish you all the happiness in the world, Lauren!'

His words were like knife slashes, and she went rigid with the pain. Even knowing that he could not possibly believe his accusations did little to mitigate the hurt. Having him angry at her for any reason, whether justified or not, made her feel isolated and afraid. She said, as steadily as she could, 'That's not fair, Shane. You have no right to insult either Jimmy or me like that when you know it's not true.'

The defiance and anger faded slowly into regret beneath the patient hurt in her eyes, and he turned away. He said quietly, after a moment, 'You're right.' And he released a stiff breath. 'I've apologised to you more than I ever have to anyone else in my life. Please accept one more.'

Her own hurt dissolved into sympathy for him. She took a step towards him. 'I know you didn't mean it,' she said softly. 'And you're not really upset with me or Jimmy, are you? It's because Jimmy reminds you so much of yourself.'

'Yes,' he admitted heavily, after a long time. Still he did not look at her. 'And because I see a kid who's about to lose everything he's got chasing rainbows and I'm the villain who's holding the pot of gold.'

'But,' she protested in some confusion, 'you said he was good. You said you would help him—you practically promised him a chart single. Wasn't any of that true?'

'Oh, yes,' agreed Shane, 'he's good. He'll probably make it. He's got a lot more going for him now than I did when I started; he might even make it to the top . . . but he's going to have to jettison a lot of unnecessary cargo along the way. Things like integrity, common sense, his family, friends, privacy, honesty . . . and one day when he looks down on all the things he's left behind and all the people he's trampled on to get to the top, he'll have me to thank for it.'

Lauren said quietly, 'Jimmy knows what he's doing. He's a very sensible young man, and he's weighed the risks. I think he can handle it.'

'Sure,' agreed Shane tonelessly. 'That's the pity, isn't it? There aren't too many people in this business who have good sense, and here's one who's ready to throw it all away. He thinks he can handle it now, but a year from now he won't know what the hell he's doing. He won't even know who he is.'

She shook her head firmly. 'It doesn't have to be that way. Give him some credit.'

After a long time he turned to look at her, and there was such sorrow in his eyes that she wanted to run to him and hold him, to comfort him even though she did not know what tormented him. 'I want to believe that,' he said. 'But I keep seeing re-runs of my own life in him, and I can't help seeing him standing in my place ten years from now, trying to tell some other kid not to make the same mistake.'

'Your only mistake,' she told him steadily, 'was in giving up.' She saw the flicker of warning in his eyes, but he no longer intimidated her. She pursued, 'You can't tell me now that the only thing missing in your life is not your music—that you wouldn't be completely happy if you were writing and singing again, performing and recording . . . you *need* that, and you can't go on punishing yourself for ever.'

He looked at her calmly. 'Maybe I am punishing myself,' he said quietly, 'but not in the way you mean, and not by choice. You see, the only thing missing in my life is love. That was part of my jettisoned cargo.'

Lauren shook her head mutely, and tears of love and yearning misted her eyes. 'No,' she whispered, touching his arm in a gesture of comfort, or entreaty, 'that's not true. You are loved . . .' her voice almost broke on the next words. 'By me.' She looked at him and all she had ever felt for him was brimming in her eyes, begging for his acceptance. 'Oh, Shane, don't you know that? I've tried to tell you, I've tried to show you . . . I love you! I was afraid before, that you would—that you wouldn't . . . but you said you wanted it, and then you turned away from me . . .' She was becoming incoherent, and the softening mixed with reluctance in his eyes only confused her more. 'I just . . . love you,' she finished, and she did not know what else to say.

There was a moment when her entire life was held in the balance by the depths of his eyes. He would either believe her or dismiss her, he would either welcome her or reject her, but she had done it, she had offered her most precious gift to him—her love. He could refuse it, but he could not give it back.

She did not know how she would survive if he refused.

And then, slowly, he pulled his arm away. That terrible hardness came over his eyes again and he said coldly, 'You don't love me, Lauren. You don't even know me.'

Her fingers found the back of a chair, she gripped it hard while slow, icy waves of pain flowed over her. She tried to speak, but the sound which escaped her tight, aching throat was not what she had intended at all. She sank to the chair, her head bowed while she struggled for control, and at last she managed thickly, 'If—I don't know you, it's because you won't give me a chance. You won't—let me know you, but you can't stop me from loving you.'

There was an endless, unbearable silence, and she could feel his eyes on her. Somehow she managed to look up at him, swallowing her pain and her pride, refusing to appear before him like a penitent child. What she saw there startled and frightened her, making her think that perhaps he was right—for this was certainly not like any part of Shane she had ever known. There was a glitter in his eyes which was as impersonal as stone, and an odd curl to his lips which was not a smile and not a grimace; it looked cruel.

'Do you want to know me, Lauren?' His voice was low, smooth, and dangerous. 'All right. Let me tell you about Shane Holt.'

He walked away from her, towards the window, and stood there looking out into the darkness as though it held endless fascination for him. He began, in a casual, almost bored tone. 'I started out a lot like Jimmy, just wanting to tell my stories and share my melodies. There was nothing naïve about me; I knew I was getting into a rough business and I thought I could handle it. For a while I did. My first single was slow to catch on, but it was a hit. I started to sell albums. Like you said, I guess that part of success came easily to me. Maybe too easily.' He fingered the curtains, Lauren watched his blurred profile in the darkened window pane with tense, silent absorption. The atmosphere in the room was heavy, threatening a violent storm. Every nerve fibre and sensor within her was alert for disaster; she could feel it but could not understand it. She knew something terrible was about to happen as, once again, her life began to change in his hands.

'But,' he picked up the story. 'I kept my head on straight. I told myself I was different, I didn't really belong to the music crowd, I was an individual and I wasn't going to be sucked down by what was happening to me ... and then, all of a sudden, I wasn't so different.' Now he was speaking mostly to himself, heavily, reflectively, each word seemed to be dragged from the centre of him with an audible pain. 'I've tried on lots of excuses . . . the pressure, the hours, the uncertainty . . . none of them really work. The truth is, it was there, it was easy, and I let it happen. I started taking pills to sleep and pills to stay awake, the usual story. I let myself be over-extended, I set up a schedule of tours and recording sessions that would have killed two men my size and age, I got a Superman complex. I forgot my old friends and didn't have time for relationships. And about that time . . .' there was a dry, brittle twist to his tone, 'I got married.'

There was a silence, and she wanted to stop him, to beg him not to put himself through this torture, not for her sake . . . but he went on. 'Do you remember a song I did,' he demanded abruptly, 'on my last album— *Tailspin into Hell*?'

Lauren nodded dully, even though he did not turn to see. That was one song which had seemed—not exactly out of character—but definitely different for him. It was haunting, tormenting, and it touched the very depths of human despair. It had told her something about him she had never really understood—or never wanted to understand. Until now.

He said, 'That was what the last two years of my career were like.' He gave a short, dry sound. 'I don't even remember writing it. I crawled out of a barbiturate stupor and found it waiting there, the words smeared all over a tablecloth, telling me what I'd lived through the night before.' Now his voice became tight, she could see his muscles knot even from that distance, and he spat out the words as though they were laced with poison. 'I'm talking about the hard life, Lauren. Waking up screaming in the middle of the night and afraid to face another day. Watching the silverware get up and walk across the table, amphetamine hangovers so bad I couldn't even hold a glass of water without breaking it or write my own name . . . Parties that lasted two or three weeks at a time, and the things that went on at those parties would turn your stomach. I'm talking about hard drugs, mainlining it, and the kind of lowlife girls like you have never even heard about. You could walk into my house any time of the day or night and find enough illegal goods to keep a narcotics squad busy for a year. Those last two years I was so stoned if you caught me on a good day I might be able to tell you my name. And I did tours, and promos, and sessions, who knows how, and half the time I didn't even know what city I was in.'

Don't, she pleaded silently, and a tear spilled over her cheek and into her parted lips. Don't go on, don't do this to yourself ... Every part of her writhed with his pain and she had to clench her hands together to stop the shaking. His suffering became hers as the sharing she had yearned for so long finally became a reality.

Shane demanded harshly, 'Do you know where I was when the baby was born?'

Again she managed to shake her head, jerkily, and tasted another tear. Again he did not see. He was a man possessed by dark demons, caught up in the spell of a nightmarish past which would only release him through the spoken word. She could not reach him; she could not help him.

'Neither do I,' he replied to her silent answer shortly. 'I woke up on my front lawn three days later feeling like I'd been hit by a truck and left in the desert to bake, and with no idea where I'd been for the past week. I didn't even see her until she was a week old, and then— I don't remember ...' His voice fell into a whisper, harsh, incredulous, torn. 'My *baby*! My child, my own flesh and blood—and I never ...' each word was dragged out with separate horror, 'even ... *knew* her!'

She heard his shaky breath, but his figure blurred hotly before her eyes. And then he squared his shoulders, staring straight out at the darkness, and went on curtly, in a rush, 'The night of the accident, we were at a friend's house. I was stoned, and planning to get even more so, but the baby started to cry and break up the party. Emily wanted to drive, but I was angry and I wouldn't let her. I thought I had it pretty well together,

I guess I'd been in worse shape and always made it home okay. The road was icy and I didn't see it. I drove like a maniac right over the side of a cliff. Not a scratch on me. You know what they say about drunks and . . .' he broke off with a sharp breath. 'When I woke up,' he finished briefly, 'I was sober, and they were dead.'

Then he turned. In his eyes was such raw agony, such fury and inner hatred that her very breathing stopped. She could not reach out to him or speak to him, nothing moved except the silent path of tears down her cheeks. Never had she seen such torment on a human face. She would not have believed it possible to withstand such pain as she felt for him in that moment. 'And that,' he said coldly, very lowly, 'is the legend of Shane Holt. A washed-out junkie and a murderer. Tell me, Lauren,' he demanded bitterly, 'who you love now.'

But, without waiting for her answer, he turned and walked out the door.

CHAPTER NINE

LAUREN could not believe she had overslept. She had lain in still agony throughout an endless night, thinking morning would never come, but like a thief slumber had crept over her in the black hours before dawn. Now morning light spilled into her eyes and made them burn, and she flung back the covers to the chill air in a bolt of panic. She had a terrible feeling that if she did not hurry she would be too late.

Throughout the night she had fought the urge to go to Shane. But she had known he would not welcome her, and she had forced herself to stay away. As she rushed haphazardly into her clothes and ran a comb through her hair she felt strongly that there was not a moment to lose.

On the stairs she found the truth in her premonition.

'Lauren!' exclaimed Jimmy happily. 'I was hoping we'd get to see you before we left.'

'L-left?' she repeated, stammering.

He nodded. 'I'm going back to Los Angeles with Shane for a little while, to work out the details and meet some people, you know ...' His face clouded a bit. 'I'd really rather be going home, of course, but ...' he smiled, 'I'd better get used to it.' He took her hand, squeezing briefly. 'We're leaving this morning and I was afraid I wouldn't get a chance to say goodbye, or to tell you—what a good friend you've been, even though we haven't known each other long.'

She hesitated, trying to adjust to the abruptness of this new information. Leaving—this morning! With no goodbye, no warning ... No, Shane would not leave her without saying goodbye. She would not let him.

Then she looked at Jimmy and wondered if she should be afraid for him. Was he really starting down that turbulent road which had led to Shane's destruction? And was it her fault? But no, she refused to accept that. She smiled at him, squeezed both his hands, and told him, 'You're going to be terrific.' Then she saw Shane standing at the bottom of the stairs.

She came slowly towards him, a fluttering in her chest overpowering the ache which had been there since last night. And in his eyes she did not see rejection, nor the awful self-hatred and reserve which had been there the night before. There was sadness, yes, and his face looked haggard, but also in some measure peaceful, resigned. He said, 'I wasn't going to leave without seeing you.'

She nodded, barely finding her voice. 'I know.'

'Will you walk with me, one more time?'

Again she nodded, and silently turned up the stairs to get her parka and her boots.

His hand moved to cover hers naturally as their footsteps crunched on the still white carpet of snow and their breath frosted the air. The sun was brilliant and cold in a pale blue sky, shadowing their footsteps with the echoes of the night before. And then she could wait no longer. She could not go on not knowing what was going on within his mind, not knowing what he might be thinking or feeling. She had to tell him . . . 'Shane,' she began anxiously, but he cut her off.

'No,' he said quietly, and through her wool gloves she felt his fingers tighten, 'I don't want you to say anything this morning. Last night was a shock and anything you say is only going to be in reaction to it—reassurance or pity.'

'No!' she gasped, but he went on.

'I've lived with this longer than you have, Lauren. Just believe me when I say it takes time. Do this one thing for me.'

But she did not need time. Nothing would change a week from now or a month from now, and the only thing which had changed last night was in her understanding of him. But she knew he would not accept anything she said in the aftermath of the storm, and because it was so important to her that he believe in her, she silently conceded his wish. She asked only, quietly, 'Why did you wait so long to tell me?'

Shane looked at her briefly. The reflection of the snow in his eyes made them look like crystal. 'Because,' he answered simply, 'I didn't have the courage to face the disappointment in your eyes when you found out the man you thought you loved was only a myth.'

'And last night,' she asked, anxiety making her voice a little breathless, 'after you told me, what did you see?'

His eyes were squinted against the brightness of the snow; he refused to answer. 'I almost didn't tell you at all,' he said at last. 'I wouldn't have, only . . .'

'Only?' she prompted, searching his face, trying to make him look at her.

'Only you became more important to me than I'd planned,' he answered flatly. 'I knew we couldn't go on this way. I'm not proud of my past,' he went on in a firmer, more decisive tone. 'But I've learned to live with it. I couldn't live any more with your not knowing.' He took a slightly unsteady breath, his eyes straight ahead, his shoulders squared. 'If you only knew,' he said lowly, 'how tempting it was to let you go on believing . . . what it was like to look into your eyes and see everything I always wanted to be but never was. Oh, sometimes you almost had me believing it myself.' But he shook it off abruptly. 'That wasn't healthy, for me or for you. The facts are what they are. I've changed, it's true, I pulled myself out of something a lot of people never escape, and I'm proud of that. But that part of my life will always be with me. I can't undo the damage, or make up for the lost time, and I think that's what hurts the most.' Her fingers tightened about his in aching support, and though there was no response from him, it seemed to encourage him to go on. 'It still haunts me day and night, Lauren,' he said roughly, refusing to look at her. 'The flashback nightmares, the temper I can't control, the loss of memory . . . knowing that I'll never be completely free of it, that I could slip any time and be right back where I was five years ago.' He took another sharp, almost painful breath. 'Two entire years completely wiped out of my life, at best only a blur of impressions and confused images. The wasted time, the lives I destroyed . . .' His voice fell. 'I can't change any of that.'

For a long time the silence was broken only by the crackle of their footsteps on a new crust of snow, and the occasional plop of a broken branch. They circled the house, and started towards the back door. And Lauren had to find the courage to ask the question she was afraid she knew the answer to already. 'Why are you leaving?'

He stopped, and looked at her. There was anguish in his eyes, but he was trying to hide it. His voice was very firm. 'It wouldn't be fair,' he said quietly. 'I can't ask you to live with my problem, even if I did have the courage to face what I would eventually begin to see in your eyes . . . disillusionment, hurt, disappointment.' She drew a quick breath, but he silenced her swiftly with a rough, 'And I can't be tempted by your fantasy any more. I wish this were a fairy tale in which we could both live happily ever after, but it just *won't work*. You would always be reminding me of what I might have been and I would always be disappointing you, and eventually we'd start to hate each other, can't you see that?' Lauren shook her head blindly, tears burning her eyes and closing her throat and turning the landscape to one nebulous blur of white agony. Why wouldn't he believe her? Why wouldn't he let her tell him that she loved him and it was forever and nothing made any difference? Only because he didn't want to hear it . . .

She heard a sound from him—of frustration, exasperation, or pain. She could not see his face through the hot film of tears and the pain inside her precluded any perception of what he might be feeling. His hand released hers. 'It's better,' he said after a time,

go against his wishes by asking Van about him. Shane had done so much for her, he had changed her life simply by touching it, and she would not repay him by pursuing him when he wanted only to be left alone. Somehow she would find a way to live with the emptiness only he could fill, for she was growing stronger every day.

'—So that's what I really called you about,' Van was saying, and she had to drag herself back to attention. 'How would you like a beautiful all-expenses-paid trip to Los Angeles for the hottest pop concert of the decade?'

Lauren smiled a little, grateful for the offer but already making excuses. Jimmy's last two letters had dealt with nothing else but the spring concert, which would be his first major performance. She had wished him luck and sent her apologies that she could not attend, but he remained adamant. It wouldn't be the same, he insisted, if she were not there to witness his debut. Apparently he had now also enlisted Van's aid. 'Oh, Van, thanks, but you know I can't——'

'No, I won't hear it. If you don't deserve a vacation who does?'

'I've only been working four months!' she laughed.

'That's long enough. You really don't mean to tell me you couldn't wrangle a week off. Because if those people don't appreciate you any more than that——'

'No, it's not that——'

'It really means a lot to Jimmy,' he insisted seriously. 'After all, if it weren't for you he wouldn't be there at all and I'll tell you the truth, honey, at this stage of a musician's career he can use all the support he can get. Besides, Marie has been fretting to see you again, and with the way you've been working it may be our last chance for a while.'

'Oh, Van, I don't know——'

'Will you at least think about it?'

'All right,' she sighed. 'I'll think about it . . .'

Three weeks later she was standing in the wings of

the especially constructed stage in Dodger Stadium behind a capacity crowd of over fifty thousand, joining in the roar of thunderous applause that accompanied the end of Jimmy Wild's first performance. 'He was terrific!' she shouted to Van, her cheeks flushed and her eyes bright. There was a swell of both pride and pathos, for she had been right—seeing him today had been like watching an updated version of Shane Holt in many ways. He did not yet have Shane's style or confidence, and his was only a reflection of the spell in which Shane Holt could hold an audience, but Shane's influence was definitely noticeable in his work. He had followed acts which had been at the top of the charts for years, but his was, to Lauren's prejudiced ears, the best performance of the day.

She laughed out loud as Jimmy leapt across the tangle of cables and equipment to swing her off her feet, crying, 'I knew you'd come! What did you think?'

He was sweaty and flushed and still charged with the adrenalin of the performance, and Lauren hugged him hard. 'You were great! Just like I knew you'd be! I wouldn't have missed it for the world.'

'Have you met my wife?' he demanded excitedly. 'How long have you been there? Did you really like it? Do you think they liked it?'

Again she laughed, squeezing his hands. His excitement was contagious, and it sparked in her eyes. 'Of course they liked it, you dummy!' She still had to shout over the continuing roar of applause. 'What do you think they're doing out there, calling for your execution? Yes, I met your wife and she's lovely—she's right over there.' Jimmy turned towards a pretty blonde woman who was waving happily at him from the other side of the stage, but before she let him go, Lauren had to insist, 'Jimmy, your material was fantastic! Did you write it? Where did you——'

There was puzzlement in his eyes as he looked over her head to Marie, and then it changed to happy anticipation. 'She doesn't know!' he exclaimed, and

Lauren was confused to see the same sparkle of secret excitement in Marie's eyes. She thought she understood, though, when Marie turned away for just a moment, then pressed a brand new record album into her hands.

'Your album!' Lauren gasped, avidly scanning it. 'I didn't know it was out yet! It looks terrific!'

'Hot off the presses,' replied Jimmy with a grin. 'Remind me to autograph it for you.' Then, glancing quickly across the stage again, he added, 'Look, I've got to go—thanks for coming! And,' he called over his shoulder with an electric look of high excitement which once again puzzled Lauren, 'look at the credits!'

But Lauren was enthralled by the cover, and she hardly heard Jimmy's parting words. The title was *Captured Dreams*, and the front cover was a photograph of exceptional quality. The picture was of a foggy hillside beneath a heavy forest of trees, and the morning light was captured in golden shafts which broke through the foliage at sparkling angles. It was so familiar to her, it was so much like the hillside upon which Shane had first kissed her that her chest tightened and a flood of memories blurred her eyes. Then Marie gently and deliberately turned the album over in her hands.

The first thing she looked for was the photo credit. 'Cover design by Shane Holt.' Her heart began to race and pound in her ears. Could it mean . . .? No, surely it meant nothing, it was just another pretty scene to him, it did not necessarily mean anything to him. Just because he got the design credit it did not necessarily mean it was even his idea, producers were always taking credit for miscellaneous aspects of an album . . . it could have been the photographer's idea, or even Jimmy's . . .

Her eyes scanned downward, anticipation tightening in her stomach and her heart pounding so hard that it actually hurt. Produced by . . . recorded at . . . back-up vocals by . . . composed by . . . 'All songs composed by Shane Holt.'

She looked slowly up at Marie, wonder widening her

eyes and a mixture of pride and pleasure and pain
swelling in her chest. He had done it! He was
composing again. After all this time . . . A sudden burst
of love so powerful it seemed to brighten the entire
world shook her, and she opened her mouth to speak,
but sudden tears flooded her throat and the words
simply would not come.

Pleasure and excitement shone in Marie's eyes, but
she laid a finger across her lips and directed Lauren's
attention to the announcer.

Lauren had not even realised that Van was no longer
with them, but it was his voice that reverberated across
the loudspeaker. She had missed most of the
introduction, and shock muted the impact of the final
words as his amplified voice echoed around her,
'—And now, for a special one-time-only appearance,
the first time on stage in five years—ladies and
gentlemen, please welcome Shane Holt!'

The dusty stage, the roar of the crowd, the lights and
the noise all receded around her. She felt Marie's
supporting hand on her arm and realised she must have
actually swayed on her feet. She couldn't move, she
couldn't speak, for a time it seemed she didn't even
breathe. And then, crossing the stage to the thunderous
swell of applause, strapping on his guitar and smiling to
the audience, was the man she loved more than life
itself.

The sudden return of awareness was so swift and
powerful it made her weak. Her heart thundered in her
throat and her limbs tingled, there was a dim ringing in
her ears and she was grateful when Marie slipped her
arm around her waist for support. Her eyes ached with
trying to get enough of him. Her head roared with
trying to believe it. He was there, in a soft suede vest
and faded jeans, dusty shafts of light falling upon his
hair and the planes of his face . . . he was there, on
stage, not twenty feet from her, and she loved him so
much she thought her heart would burst.

Hot tears of pride and yearning flooded her eyes and

she had to continuously blink them away for fear of missing just one second of him. She thought the applause and shouts of encouragement would go on for ever, but then Shane spoke into the microphone and, as always, his effect on the audience was immediate. A respectful, anticipatory hush fell over the crowd.

'This is a very special time for me,' he said, and the magic of his voice fell over the crowd like a soothing draught. Each word was a gentle echo, simple, concise, without pretension. 'And this song is for a very special lady—the woman who brought music back into my life.' Marie's arm tightened about Lauren's waist, but she hardly noticed. Her head was whirling and she tried to focus on Shane, hardly daring to believe it, straining for some sign or signal, filling her senses with him, afraid that if she blinked he might evaporate before her eyes. He finished simply, 'It's called *Morning Song*,' and he signalled with an almost imperceptible nod to the back-up musicians as the first strains of the melody began.

> Dawn answers gently
> the night's lonely cry,
> spilling like tears on the sill . . .
> Whispering melodies
> yet to be sung
> And you are the reason
> morning has come . . .

The music carried her away and left her weak, it filled every fibre of her being with love and joy. It far transcended anything Shane had ever done both in style and sophistication, making his earlier works pale by comparison. It was haunting, it was moving, it filled the stage with sunshine and glory, it was all he had ever been and all she had always known he could be—it was what the two of them, together, were. But beyond even his mastery of the art was the meaning behind its creation. Through the music he spoke to her, it was an exclusive communication only they could share expressing what he felt for her and what she felt for him. '*You are the reason morning has come* . . .'

When the last chords died away tears of love and joy and pride were flowing uncontrollably down her cheeks. For just a moment there was an entranced silence from the crowd, and then the stadium burst into a wild roar of applause. Then Shane turned, and his eyes met hers. He crossed the stage towards her.

The moments between them seemed endless. Colours and movements streaked together before her running vision and the sounds of adulation from the crowd dimmed, for it was only the two of them alone in the crowded backstage area, nothing intruded on this moment.

Then suddenly his hands were upon her arms, there was confusion and alarm in his face and he whispered anxiously, 'Lauren—darling, I didn't mean to make you cry. I didn't mean to upset you. What——'

But she only shook her head violently, and radiance beamed through her tears as she looked at him, trying to drink it all in at once as love and happiness swept over her in reverberating waves. 'Shane, I——' But the words were choked back on a gulping sob of pure joy, and a measure of relief crossed his face as he seemed to understand.

His hands tightened on her arms as his eyes swept the crowded area impatiently. 'Come over here,' he said hoarsely, and pulled her around equipment and props and road managers shouting orders to a relatively unoccupied corner of the wings. 'I have to talk to you——'

But the love that flooded her could be contained no longer. 'Don't talk,' she whispered, and her arms were about his neck, her lips meeting his in a kiss of urgency and soaring joy. His hands pressed into her back and he kissed her with a barely restrained desperation, a wonder and a growing need that strained to make her a part of him and to never let her go. His lips were on her face and her eyes, brushing against her hair, then his

warm breath was streaming over her neck and his arms
crushed her as he whispered unsteadily, 'Oh, Lauren, I
love you. I love you so much.'

Once again she caught a sob of wonder and
happiness in her throat and she pressed her face into his
shoulder, tightening her arms about him until the
muscles ached. The powerful embrace could not be
maintained for long, and in a moment Shane loosened
his hold and took a small step backwards, his eyes
scanning her face with a brilliant urgency of wonder
and joy. 'I have to talk to you——'

'Why didn't you call me?' she began at the same time,
then she laughed a little, foolishly and happily,
scrubbing at her wet face with the back of her hand.

He offered her a handkerchief and smiled down at
her indulgently, stroking her hair with a slightly
unsteady hand. 'Will you please stop crying?' he
suggested. 'You're making me think I've done
something wrong.'

'Nothing wrong,' she gulped, pressing the handkerchief over her face. 'Everything—right. I can't stop
crying. I'm too happy!'

His lips tightened in a familiar affectionate smile.
'Typical female logic!' And then suddenly he gathered
her in his arms again, simply holding her, his indrawn
breath swift and urgent against her ear, every muscle in
his body straining with the need for her. He pressed his
lips against her forehead sweetly and gently, and once
again wrapped his arms about her, holding her as
though to never let her go. 'Oh, Lauren,' he said
rapidly, 'don't you know how long I've loved you? But
it was so complicated. I think I began to love you that
night you told me I was an emotional monster . . . no
one has ever cared enough about me to tell me the plain
truth before, no one has ever been able to make me see
it so clearly. But I had nothing to offer you—how can
you know the torture I went through? Loving you,
afraid of disappointing you, wanting to get closer to
you and hating it when you backed away—hating

myself for daring to love you and afraid to believe it as true, dreading the day when you found out I wasn't really the man you thought but loving you so much I had to take the chance . . .'

She pushed away, her eyes shining with defiance and sincerity, urgency propelling to her lips the words she had for so long yearned to say. 'Oh, Shane, I've tried to tell you . . . it's not the music or the musician that I love—it's the soul of the man who created the music. They *are* one and the same, they always will be. I love your beauty and your simplicity and your courage, your honesty and your strength and—your weakness. I love you because you reach me when no one else can, and you touch me in places no one ever has before, you're like the other half of me. Please can't you see it's not what you've done that matters, but who you are? That's what I can't stop loving!'

But almost before the words were finished their lips were together, hungrily reaching for each other, exploding in wild joy and ultimate relief and final contentment. All barriers slipped away and only they were left, true and complete, loving each other. Waves of passion swelled and dipped, and finally evened out into a wondrous joy that stretched endlessly before them, waiting to be explored at depth.

'Lauren,' Shane whispered at last against her face, 'I had to leave, you understand that, don't you? I had to get rid of all the ghosts that haunted me before I could ask you to share my life.'

She looked up at him in pure and quiet adoration. 'And you've done that?'

He nodded. 'With the first song I wrote for Jimmy. You were right all along, Lauren, composing is what I need, it's where I belong.'

She looked past him towards the stage, where even now another act was setting up. 'Your performance was beautiful,' she said softly. And she looked at him. 'But you didn't have to do it, you know. Not to prove anything to me.'

'I did it,' he told her seriously, 'as a gesture of respect to you. And to prove something to myself.'

'And,' she asked almost hesitantly, searching his face, 'did you?'

'Yes.' His smile was quiet and loving. 'I proved that I could do it—not because I had to, but because I wanted to. I'm not going back on tour, Lauren. I may record again, just once in a while, but mostly what I want to do is write.' His smile deepened with tenderness. 'I have so many love songs inside me now it will take forever just to write them all down.'

Wordlessly, she stepped into his arms and they held each other for a long time, needing no words to communicate the depth of their feelings. There was a smile in his voice as he brushed her hair with a kiss and enquired, 'Will you?'

She looked up at him. 'Will I what?'

His eyes were deep with adoration and the quiet confidence of the answer he knew she would give. 'Share my life with me.'

'Yes,' she smiled. 'Oh yes!' And she stepped back into his arms—the only place she had ever belonged.

THE WALTZ KING OF VIENNA

Johann Strauss, Lauren's *second*-favorite composer, was known throughout nineteenth-century Europe as the "Waltz King." The Viennese composer of the famous "Blue Danube," Strauss created hundreds of waltzes, polkas and quadrilles that swirled dancers of Vienna and the world.

Yet music was once forbidden fruit to Johann, who was born in 1825 and raised near the shores of the Danube. His father, a famous musician and composer, insisted that banking was a more reputable vocation for his son. His mother, however, sensing innate musical talent, secretly supplied young Johann with a violin and lessons. One day his father, home from touring, found Johann practicing in front of a mirror, moving as he himself did on stage. Appalled Strauss senior grabbed the violin and locked it away. His mother bought another violin with her household money the very next day. Johann never practiced at his parents' home again!

At nineteen, in his first public performance, Johann captivated the audience with his original waltzes. Carried triumphantly from the stage on the shoulders of his jealous father's fans, he began a career that lasted more than fifty years. With billowing dark hair and a bow held primly in his fingertips, Johann toured Europe, and in 1872 joined in a celebration of world peace at the International Peace Jubilee in Boston, Massachusetts. While *musikdirektor* for the Austrian imperial court balls, he hobnobbed with the Habsburgs, who found that his music reflected the elgance and *joie de vivre* of prosperous Vienna.

His passion for music was shared by his loving first wife. Empty after her death, he married a young woman who later caused him grief. After a painful divorce, Johann found happiness with his third wife until the end of his days in 1899. And for people like Lauren, who loved to listen to his lilting melodies, his music lives on.

Discover the new and unique

Harlequin Category-Romance Specials!

Regency Romance	Gothic Romance	Romantic Suspense
A DEBT OF HONOR	THE SATYR RING	THE SEVENTH GATE
Mollie Ashton	Alison Quinn	Dolores Holliday
THE FAIRFAX BREW	THE RAVENS	THE GOBLIN TREE
Sara Orwig	OF ROCKHURST	Robyn Anzelon
	Marian Martin	

A new and exciting world of romance reading

Harlequin Category-Romance Specials

Available wherever paperback books are sold, or send your name, address and zip or postal code, along with a check or money order for $2.25 for each book ordered (include an additional total of 75¢ postage and handling), payable to Harlequin Reader Service, to:
Harlequin Reader Service

In the U.S.
P.O. Box 52040
Phoenix, AZ 85072-9988

In Canada
649 Ontario Street
Stratford, Ontario N5A 6W2

CR-100

Harlequin Presents

ALL-TIME FAVORITE BESTSELLERS
...love stories that grow
more beautiful with time!

Now's your chance to discover the earlier great books in Harlequin Presents, the world's most popular romance-fiction series.

Choose from the following list.